SON OF CENTAURY ZEBRA

JACQUI SIMON

PublishAmerica
Baltimore

First printing

ISBN: 1-4137-6842-3
PUBLISHED BY PUBLISHAMERICA, LLLP
www.publishamerica.com
Baltimore

Printed in the United States of America

DEDICATION:

This book is for those closest to me: my little brother, who gave me ideas; my mom, who's never failed to support me; my sister, who's always been there for me; my older brother, whose perseverance is like no other; and to my friends

Thank you all for the love!

Candice,
thankyou for
being a friend!
Jacqui

CHAPTER ONE

Captain Casper Marseille Hawk scratched the top of his head and slumped down in his command chair. Exasperated at the last few days of non-stop combat in the Achilles quadrant, he was tired, *really* tired. All he wanted now was a hot shower and his bed on his home planet of Hearth Condes, something which seemed to be an impossible goal at the moment, because of the amount of ships trying to be coordinated by one small station orbiting the planet.

"I say again, Command Central, this is the battle squadron Centaury Zebra. I do not care what in the hell else you've got going on right now, I have twenty-two ships that haven't seen home in eight months! So either tell us which platforms to set down on or just stop telling me what I can and cannot do!" Casper hissed.

The bridge crew around him were doing their best to hide their snickering faces and smiles as their captain sounded like he was ready to burst. The com-link opened up again from the space station.

"Negative, Centaury Zebra, we've got six civilian transports that came in before you, two of which are carrying diplomats for the celebrations tonight. If you honestly think you take priority over them, then maybe you'd like to tell them yourself that they have to take a back seat," came the rude reply. This time Casper stood up, livid at the way he was being spoken to.

"THEN GIVE ME THEIR FREQUENCY!!!" he exclaimed.

"Negative, Centaury Zebra, hold on and you'll be dealt with in the order you came."

"Son of a bitch," Casper mumbled as he sat back in his chair.

"Maybe we should just go around the planet in an intimidating circle." Casper looked to his right hand where, at the security console, his second in command and good friend Commander Sean-Patrick Harper raised a notorious eyebrow. Casper gave a short tired laugh and shook his head, then he had an idea. He smiled wickedly and mischievously, then stood up and walked over to Harper's console. When he started pushing buttons, Harper's eyes went huge and his mouth dropped open.

"WHAT ARE YOU DOING??" he exclaimed. Casper simply patted Harper on the shoulder and stood up looking at his communications officer.

"Ensign, open up a link to the other ships please," he asked ever so nicely. By this point everyone was looking at Harper, who was nearly crying with laughter.

"Link established, sir," Ensign Linda Park said.

"All ships, this is your commander speaking, lock all weapons on the command station…let's see if we can get their attention." Casper smiled wryly. Laughter erupted over the line and seconds later Harper confirmed that all ships had done as ordered. It took mere seconds for the command station to contact Casper's ship.

"We're uh…being hailed, sir." Linda laughed. He nodded to her to open up the frequency then stood proudly at his chair.

"Command Central ready to help us so soon?" Casper asked innocently.

"CENTAURY ZEBRA, STAND DOWN!! STAND DOWN!! You will be considered hostile should you refuse to comply."

"Negative, Command Central, this is going to end in one of two ways: one, you give us a platform to land on and we'll be on our way, or two, I blow your ass up and *take* a platform to land on," Casper said. There was a moment of silence, minus the laughter coming from his bridge crew, and then all of a sudden there was a bright explosion off the port bow that knocked Casper back into his seat.

"Holy shit…I think they just fired at us…" Harper said in disbelief.

"They WHAT???" Casper bellowed. He was about to have a few choice words with the command when a different voice than before came over the link.

"You don't scare anyone down here. Casper…well, save the operator you practically made piss his pants but other than that…Keep your damn shirt on and stand down, we'll get to you in a second…bitch," said a wry voice. Casper was speechless and was sure he looked quite the fool with his face in a dumbfounded look.

Harper on the other hand was in tears and was starting to stand down the weapons.

"Oh man…I didn't even know he was going to be on the station!" Harper laughed. Casper just sat in his chair in silence. Time and time again something like this had happened, and he hated the man responsible each time. Maverick Bruce Avery Hawk, Casper's older brother had been a pain in the ass since day one. This time was no different. Casper knew everyone was laughing at him and he hated it, just like he hated his older brother.

He got to his feet and with a straight face looked at Linda, who was laughing along with the others.

"Patch a secure line through to my captain's room, Ensign," he said. Linda could see he was upset and bit her tongue as she nodded and did as ordered. Quickly Casper headed into his private room and sat behind his desk ready to take the call through his computer screen.

"Call's coming through, sir," Linda said over the com. Casper clenched his jaw but composed himself to face his brother. Maverick's face appeared on the computer screen sporting a smug, proud-of-himself smile.

"Hey, little bro, what's up?" he asked.

"You damn well know what's up! You made me look stupid in front of my entire squadron! I need to have their respect, Maverick, and you just killed that! Four months I've been in battle with these men and women, whom I have been with for several years, and you threw it all out the window in five minutes!" Casper fumed. Maverick rolled his eyes, smiled, and looked down at his hands.

"Aw come on, Cass, it was a joke, you need to take it as such. You haven't lost anything because of it. Lighten up, buddy," he replied. But Casper wasn't about to lighten up, he had been embarrassed and he felt stupid.

"You're just jealous that I'm in control of the squadron, and all mom and dad gave you was home security," Casper sneered. Again Maverick laughed as if it were nothing at all, annoying Casper even more. All he wanted to do at this point was anger his brother, get under his skin like Maverick had managed to do with him. The plan seemed to be a failure, however, like usual, as Maverick seemed just as cool as normal.

"Cass, I'm home security because I'm going to be in charge of this planet one day. They want me to learn my place as you have to learn yours with the squadron. I know what you're trying to do, and I'm telling you now, it isn't going to work. You're a good kid, Casper, and I'm proud of you. So can we talk about tonight? Your dress uniform has been added to—nice lovely medals on it now because of the Achilles Campaign. How'd that go by the way?" Maverick asked. Casper's knuckles were turning white with anger; his brother managed to belittle everything he did, and it sickened him to no end. Especially now after the past eight months that he had been through.

The war was a senseless one and completely unnecessary in his eyes; a war that had been going on since before he was born. The universe just wasn't big enough apparently for humans with different views to live peacefully. It never made sense as to exactly why differences couldn't be settled, but then again, when it came down to religion and power mankind was notorious for forcing their beliefs on others.

Power and faith was the motto of Centaury Zebra, and despite Casper's dislike of the idea, he followed like a good prince. As was his title and duty, he was born royalty; his mother the eldest of her family was given the title of Sovereign Ruler of Hearth Condes. After which she was wed to the general of the military's first son, thus bringing the military and home security under one power. It was an unplanned union of powers as Casper's mom and dad had simply been two people madly in love with each other.

In a way, Casper had always seen himself as the black sheep of the family, because he never had a choice and he loathed the fact that his sole purpose was to fight wars. It always seemed like when he was with his family he was never really *with* them. Maverick and his mom and dad always got along much more than he did with the three of them. He was alone in a universe filled with humans and today was no different. Maverick was the oldest and his parents' favorite. Casper knew that and accepted it, but it still hurt to think they always seemed to *care* more about what Maverick was doing and not him.

When Casper had left eight months ago his parents had seen him off, but it was very brief as Maverick needed their opinion on a diplomatic situation that he had been put in charge of. Casper was sent off to war and the possibility of losing his life, but mom and dad had cut short the goodbye.

Casper shook the thoughts from his head. He was a soldier; it was his job to die for his planet, as it was his brother's to lead the people at home. The thought that he wouldn't be missed should he be killed was a sad, pessimistic one, but the truth.

"Cass? What's wrong?" Maverick's voice was more serious now, it almost sounded like there was concern in it. Casper looked up at the screen, took a deep breath, and kept the stoic look on his face that he was accustomed to showing.

"We lost two cruisers, 2000 souls, I spent the last two days of our voyage home writing their families," Casper said as if it were nothing. Maverick's face was suddenly filled with sorrow and regret.

"I'm sorry, that couldn't have been easy," he said. Casper raised an eyebrow, masking his true feelings.

"That's war, Maverick. It happens, people die, were you really expecting different? Oh wait, I forgot, you prefer not to get involved; diplomacy is best right? What I'm doing isn't that important to a politician like you," he replied with a laugh. He wanted it to sound as if it didn't matter to a battle-hardened man such as himself. It was clear by Maverick's face he wasn't buying it at all; after all, Casper was only twenty-seven years old but had responsibilities far beyond that.

"Cass, don't pretend like you don't think everyone doesn't care what happens to you. You mean a lot to a lot of people…"

"Spare me, Maverick, and don't call me Cass, I'm not a kid anymore. Captain Hawk out." With that Casper cut the channel before Maverick could reply. He was tired of talking to him anyway, tired of having fake pity bestowed on him by his brother. He leaned back in his chair and ran his hands through his hair. Two thousand people…*two-thousand* had been killed, countless others had been injured, including himself when a warring ship had nearly collided with them. Casper had spent a week in the infirmary with a broken leg, a nasty gash on his side that stretched from his waist to his arm pit, and then there was the very prominent scar tracing from the corner of his mouth to his right temple.

He managed to keep it hidden like he had with his brother over com links by slightly turning his head to the right. His family had yet to see him with his new scars and slower pace because of his leg. The bone, although healed, had done so slightly crooked, hence the slight limp. He had to try and walk slower to avoid having people stare.

"Captain, we've been given landing coordinates," Harper called.

"Good. Tell the other ships to proceed, we'll be the last ones to set down," Casper replied. He felt the ship shudder slightly as it fell back in formation to set down on the planet. On the one hand, he was happy to be home because it meant he could finally relax and not worry if his ship was moments away from being space junk. On the other hand, Casper would become the shadow on the wall like his entire life and cease to be the prominent figure he was during battle. The only thing he had to hold onto was the fact that soon enough he'd be sent out to face another battle.

An hour later Casper was back in his room of the palace, a room he always thought was too big for his preference. He sat at his desk going over the debrief he was going to send to the counsel of the events in Achilles when there was a double chime at his door.

"Enter," he called. He kept his head down at his panel not really wanting the interruption.

"Enter? My, haven't we become formal," Maverick said. Casper glanced up briefly and then went back to his work. His brother was dressed in his royal uniform, clean cut, face nicely shaven, looking like a king or as the eldest prince should.

"Imagine that, some people grow up," he remarked.

"Cass, what's up with you? You seem so distant," Maverick replied.

"I've got work to do before dinner, Maverick, what do you want? And I told you to stop calling me Cass, I'm not six years old anymore," Casper said.

"Okay, Casper, excuse me Captain Hawk, may I request an audience?" Maverick asked. With a heavy sigh Casper put down his work and looked up at Maverick. His brother's face faltered slightly. "Wow, they told me you had been injured, but…that's one hell of a scar," he said.

"Is that why you're here? To check on my disfigurements?" Casper asked. Maverick sat down across from Casper and looked at him very seriously.

"No, Casper, it's not. I came because you've been gone for eight months and I wanted to make sure you're alright," he replied. Casper rolled his eyes and shook his head with a laugh.

"Spare me, Maverick, you're here because you're being diplomatic; it's what you do to make sure you don't have any enemies. Don't worry, brother, you needn't fear me, I'm just a shadow on the wall," he said.

"Are you that afraid to be back with your friends and family?" Maverick asked.

"Not afraid, tired. And as for friends, my friends are on the ship I just stepped off of, so if there is nothing else, I'll see you at dinner," Casper replied. He looked back to his work and started going over it again only to have the pad pulled out of his hand. It was a violent act that startled Casper. He looked up at his brother incredulously and stood up. He refused to be threatened by anyone, let alone his older brother.

"What is your problem?" Maverick asked.

"Me? Put down my information pad and threaten me again, then I'll show you what my problem is and I'll deal with it too," Casper hissed. His brother stepped back and put the pad down immediately putting his hands up in surrender.

"Casper, what's happened to you?" Maverick asked incredulously. "You used to be…"

"What, Maverick? What? Quiet, obedient, whipped? I'm a soldier, a damn good one too and…" Before Casper could finish he stopped himself and looked away with a sigh. "Things have changed is all, I'm just exhausted." He realized that creating an enemy over the one man he'd be forced to work with for the rest of his life wasn't a good idea. He sat back down heavily and took back his pad and started working again.

"Maybe you should get some shut eye before dinner," Maverick suggested. Casper shook his head.

"A half hour isn't enough time to recover eight months, Mav, nor is it enough time to make it to the dinner tonight dressed properly. So if you don't mind…" he said.

"Yeah I do, stop trying to get rid of me, Cass. We're supposed to be brothers. Now, royalty or not, we have a duty to each other to…" Casper burst out laughing. He laughed so hard his side ached. "What's so funny?" Maverick asked.

"You!" Casper bellowed. "We have a name for guys like you on the ships: Public Puppets, because nothing you do or say is from your own mind, it's all what you believe the public want to hear. Really Mav, you should hear yourself sometimes." He stopped laughing, however, when his brother slammed his hand down on the desk. Another violent act, one which now definitely had Casper on guard. It was almost as if a switch had been installed in his brain and whenever something violent happened it was switched on and in defensive mode.

"Damn it, Casper, I'm trying to be your friend! That shit you pulled today charging weapons at the command station was stupid. So fine, you want me not to be diplomatic, you want me to give it to you straight up? Our parents are pissed at you because you did something so stupid. I came in here to soften the blow but fine, you're going to be an ass, then so am I. You fucked up, Cass, you fucked up royal with that stunt and you set a bad example for everyone under your command! You'll have to explain yourself to a lot of people tonight, and I'm not going to protect your ass as per usual," Maverick exclaimed.

"What's that supposed to mean?"

"Some of the reports from the conflict were questioned many times by the counsel. Every time I backed you, I convinced them you did everything properly, but I'm not going to do it anymore," Maverick replied. Casper was furious and came around his desk so as to stand face to face with the man.

"Good! Because I never asked you to! I never asked for that nor did I ask to be born into this stupid family, nor did I wish to return from the Achilles quadrant minus two ships!"

"Something you'll have to explain in great detail, the counsel didn't take the loss of two ships lightly, Cass, not at all," Maverick said. Suddenly Casper felt betrayed by his supposed family.

"Get out," Casper growled. His voice was low and threatening, and it clearly had an effect on Maverick.

"Casper, I'm sorry, really, I am. I've been taking a lot of flack recently for…well whatever, but I do know Mom and Dad want to talk to you before the banquet," he said. Casper was still set on defend and didn't like what he was hearing.

"Get out…" he growled again. Maverick, however, didn't move, he stood his ground.

"Come on, Cass, don't be like this, just talk to Mom and Dad, that's all they want…" Casper snapped, he didn't care what his parents wanted or anyone else for that matter, what about what *he* wanted? What about what *he* was dealing with right now? Two thousand people he had lost, people who had trusted him with their lives.

"GET OUT!!!" Casper screamed, his voice louder than he had meant it to be and twice as threatening. Maverick stumbled backward toward the door almost knocking a chair over. His face was filled with...*fear?* Never before had Casper instilled anything more than annoyance in his older brother, but he was positive that was what he was seeing in his brother's eyes.

"Casper, please, you need to talk to..."

"LEAVE ME ALONE!!!" Casper yelled again. This time he picked up the chair Maverick had almost tripped over as he advanced closer to the door and tossed it aside like it were nothing. It hit a light, which smashed, sending sparks everywhere, but he didn't give it a second look. He had his eyes locked on his brother almost as if he drew something on the emotion of fear. As a soldier it was the one emotion you could count on to figure out what was going to happen next. People who were scared were predictable and usually did whatever you convinced them was the safest course of action.

"I'm going, Casper, but I'll be around if you need someone to..." Maverick's voice was slightly shaky and less filled with the self-assurance it had before.

"I don't need anyone, especially not people pretending to know who I am! If I have to tell you to get out of my face one more time, so help me God you will be the main course at the banquet tonight," Casper replied. The look of fear in Maverick's eyes had some sorrow to it, but it didn't matter as soon he slipped out of the room and closed the door behind him.

Casper was breathing heavily, command of a squadron had changed him a great deal. He had been part of combat situations since he was sixteen and was no stranger to war, but this Achilles battle was the first that he had been in charge of so many lives. Over the past eight months he had developed a strict regiment to keep himself in top shape, subsequently committing social suicide. While others had a drink after shift or ate a meal with friends, Casper had been working out making sure he was strong enough to fight off anything in and out of a pressure suit as was required sometimes when the battle became close quarters on the hull of a ship. His hair was also much longer not for lack of caring, but he never had time or felt it important enough to get it cut. It was a tangled mess of hair that was just below his shoulder line. He always managed to keep the black shaggy mess in a tight pony tail, which he thought gave him a look of distinction.

There were, of course, the scars he sported from the eight-month battle that were almost reminders of who he was now and who he used to be. In a strange way, he took pride in his scars and even the limp in some aspects because it was a testament to the fact that he wasn't a soft-skinned prince as some may have seen him as a child but a fierce warrior not afraid of a fight.

His only regret was the fact that he was still a prince and still had to conform to the politics of that title. A role which made it impossible for many to whom he had to answer, to appreciate his soldier qualities.

Casper walked over to his dresser and pulled out his freshly pressed uniform with two new medals on it. In total he had eleven lacing his left lapel. He hated showing off like the royal uniform did but knew if he showed up to the banquet in a combat uniform or worse a simple robe he'd never hear the end of it from the entire planet. Imagine a prince wanting to be comfortable in what he was wearing! Shame on him!

He smiled as he stripped to his skivvies and went to take a shower before adorning the stiff uniform with the collar that he affectionately referred to as his choke chain.

Later that evening Casper sat at a large table beside his mother, father, and brother; it was the head table in the banquet hall filled with hundreds of men and women from the large cities around the world. Casper's father, Anthony Hawk, smiled at his wife, Patricia, who was giving a speech to the lords and ladies of the room. At a second main table in front and on a lower level from the head table was the table where the members of the counsel sat. Eight men and women who answered to Casper's parents on all issues regarding the planet's safety and politics.

When the room started clapping Casper snapped out of his trance of casing the room only to realize everyone was looking at him. He realized his mother had introduced him to speak of the recent campaign he had returned from. That's when it happened; he stood to speak and realized he had nothing to say, what could he say? Hundreds of people were staring at him, waiting intently ready to hang on his every word, and he had nothing to say. Just as he thought he'd die of embarrassment his mother stood again looking out to the crowd.

"You must forgive the prince as he is only home mere hours and probably has not had much rest. I must apologize as I think I've caught my poor son off guard!" she said. The room erupted in laughter and yet again it was at his expense. Suddenly he found his voice.

"Actually, lords and ladies, I was trying to find the correct words to tell you of the battle I have just returned from," he said. Patricia looked at him and nodded with a smile then sat down. Casper looked at his family and then out onto the crowd, "Unfortunately, it did not go as well as expected," he said.

"Isn't it true you secured the Achilles quadrant borders between us and the enemy?" Someone asked. Casper thought it was one of the members of the counsel, so he looked at them when he spoke.

"Yes, but two ships were destroyed in the process. I lost very good men and women out there, and I refuse to see a good side to that. I stand here before you all tonight not to explain my actions but to tell you of the men and women who we should all be thinking of tonight," he said. Anthony raised his glass and soon the rest of the room followed.

"To those brave, heroic lost souls," he said. A chorus of "here, here" rang out as Casper sat back down in his chair. He had wanted to say more, actually a lot more. He wanted to scold everyone there for looking so happy and content with the way they lived. He wanted them to suffer as the men and women who died under his command had suffered.

Beside him, once the dinner began, his mother leaned over to him and spoke quietly.

"Maverick told me you two had an argument and you didn't seem yourself, are you alright, dear?" she asked. Casper looked up at her and abandoned forking his food around his plate.

"After eight months of no contact my family still thinks they know what I should seem like? Forgive me, Mother, I don't mean to be rude, but I'm fine," he replied.

"That is why you haven't touched your food and have barely cracked a smile all night?" she asked. Casper simply shook his head and pushed his plate away from him.

"I've lost my appetite, Mother," he said. Patricia frowned and looked at him, her deep blue eyes filled with concern.

"You never used to call me 'mother' it makes me sound so old," she said. "And believe it or not I do care for you and your well-being." The urge to get up and toss his plate across the room was growing, but instead Casper stood up.

"That's why when we said goodbye you never said come home safe, you simply gave me a hug and said bye…Christ, Mother, you didn't even wish me luck before running off to help Maverick!" he exclaimed. "Again forgive me but I need some air." With a swift kick of his heels Casper made his way from the banquet hall out into the cool night air.

He sucked it in like he had been suffocated in that room by some oversized pillow. Already was he getting restless and felt he needed to get back on his ship the Spector and take off into the wilds of space.

"You sure do know how to give one hell of a death glare." Casper turned away from the balcony edge and saw Harper in dress uniform.

"Sean, I didn't even realize you were here," he said as he shook the man's hand.

"It's a big crowd in there, I'm surprised I even managed to see you from the crappy table the crew and I are sitting at," Harper replied. Casper stood up straighter and cocked his head to the side.

"The crew? Who's here with you?" he asked.

"Lt Ryan Keeper, Cmdr. Danielle Tyson, and we managed to sneak in Ensign Park and Ensign Maddox past security; they wanted to eat like a royal, so we brought them along. Hell, I wasn't even planning on coming to this schmooze fest, you know what politics does to me," Harper replied. Casper smiled and nodded. Keeper was his trusted head engineer. He, Harper, and Cmdr. Tyson, captain of the second ship in formation with the squadron were the only people he really considered his friends. His communications ensign and his flight ensign were also close but only to the extent that their ranks would allow. Still Casper saw Linda and Freddy as more of family than his real one.

"You're lucky, you come here and people see a soldier; I come here and people see a prince who knows what in the hell they are talking about when it deals with the planet." He sighed. "I'm glad you guys are here actually, what's say we get out of here and find a bar?"

"No can do, Prince." Harper sighed. "As fun as that sounds, I was put on security detail."

"What?" Casper asked. "You're military, homeland isn't your turf; besides, why would you agree to something so stupid as guarding a bunch of stiffs?"

"I'm not guarding the banquet, your parents put me on *your* guard duty. Apparently your family has been getting threats, and they know how you like running off like the black sheep that you are..." Harper replied.

"Stop, Sean, okay, stop, I don't want to hear it. So you're telling me you came because you had to?" Casper asked. He felt almost crushed at the fact that a man he thought was his friend was only at the banquet because he received an order to. However, Harper shook his head.

"I'm here because of something you said when we were still in the Achilles quadrant," he replied.

"What did I say?" Casper asked.

"You said and I quote, 'when we get back and you see me in a uniform that screams tool, shoot me because you'll be putting me out of my misery.' Of course, I believe you were very drunk and tired at the time," Harper said. "So I have my weapon already to burn a hole through you...shall we do it now or wait until after the dinner?" For a few seconds Casper didn't know what to say, but then he started laughing and patted his friend on the back.

"Aw man, what would I do without you?" He sighed.

"I figure not a whole hell of a lot," Harper came back causing Casper to laugh even harder.

When he calmed down he turned back to the hall he had just exited and sighed.

"I should get back in there, appearances and all," he said.

"This is true," Harper replied. "On the plus side they should be serving dessert right about now." Casper shook his head and walked beside Harper back into the building. Even though nothing had been said on the subject, Casper knew Harper had come out there to make sure he was okay. It was very much appreciated that he didn't ask the same question but rather eased the mood. Had Casper felt like sharing anything, he was sure it would be to a man like Harper who was always there for him.

"You're a good man, Harper, a good man," Casper said.

"That's what the ladies say." Harper smiled as he wiggled his eyebrows.

When they got back to the banquet Casper said goodbye to his friend and rejoined his family at the head of the table. This time it was his father who approached him and put his hand on Casper's shoulder.

"I'm sure losing those ships wasn't easy, but I'm proud of you son," Anthony said. Casper looked at him.

"You've been talking to Mom and Maverick haven't you? Well before you ask, I am fine, just tired," he said. "Give me a day and I'll be back on my feet."

"Good man." Anthony nodded. He then returned to his seat and started chatting with his wife. Casper, in the meanwhile, rolled his eyes at the faked, forced attention he was getting from his family. He didn't like it; being patronized was never pleasant.

While the room was abuzz with chatter, Casper lost interest in the goings on and started thinking of how he would spend his first free day in over thirty-two weeks. Somehow he felt the lake calling his name and maybe some horseback riding on the trails of the pinewood forest. Possibly some target practice...Casper stopped himself; guns, he was still thinking of guns, and perfecting his use of them. He really was a war-hardened soldier and in some ways he hated himself for his tactical mind. Everything, it seemed, he would do or say recently came down to tactics and logistics.

He managed to spot his friends sitting at a table way on the other side of the room, they were chatting animatedly and looked like they were having a good time. Casper wondered what had been said when they all burst out laughing and wished he was part of the conversation. However, he had a title to represent and that was something he couldn't let go no matter how much he wanted to.

After dinner Casper stood at the exit of the hall, dutifully wishing the patrons a goodnight and thanking them for coming. Opposite him was the rest of his family, so fortunately he only had to speak to few people. Everyone else radiated toward his older brother with comments of praise for how he's turning out and what a fine young man he's grown into. Casper shook his head as yet another lord came to give all praise to Maverick and was about to make a break for his room when a woman came up to him.

The woman was dressed in the finest clothing Casper had ever seen on a woman, she was gorgeous and her blonde hair was tightly wrapped in some sort of purple shawl. She was slightly shorter than Casper and her slender figure was accented by a very striking deep blue short dress. The whole outfit was finished off with knee-high boots that looked very comfortable.

"Prince Casper, it's a pleasure to finally meet you," she said. Casper took her hand as he had done several times that night with all the ladies of the court and kissed it.

"The pleasure is all mine," he said dutifully. To his surprise the woman giggled and took her hand back.

"Really, sir, that's hardly necessary you don't need to treat me like you do the civvies." She smiled. Casper was surprised, the way she was speaking was almost military.

"I'm sorry do I know you?" Casper asked.

"Not really, I guess I didn't really expect you to." She smiled shyly. She appeared to be sad that he didn't know who she was, but he really couldn't place the face.

"What's your name?" he asked.

"Isis Soul," she replied. Then it came to him, the first name didn't ring a bell but the last name did. Soul, he had seen that name on a list somewhere but where he couldn't remember. He did know, however, she was military but where she served and who she served for he didn't know.

"You're military," he said. She nodded.

"I was on the *Magellan*," she replied. Casper looked at her seriously and raised an eyebrow. The *Magellan* had been one of the two ships destroyed in the conflict, she and all her crew had been destroyed.

"How is that possible?" he asked.

"Because of yourself, sir; actually, when the Specter got hit pretty bad she needed extra crewmen to fix her. I was on that list, fortunately." Isis shrugged. Casper suddenly realized where he had seen that name before. When he had been injured in the infirmary he could do nothing more than go over reports from all the repairs going on. He remembered that the name Soul had come up a lot. She was good at what she did and signed off on a lot of repairs.

"You got my ship back on her toes almost single-handedly," Casper said. Isis smiled and blushed slightly.

"I'd hardly say that, sir." She smiled. "I just finished faster than some of the others, after *The Magellan* was destroyed...well, you could say I wanted to lose myself in my work. I lost a lot of friends that day." Casper closed his eyes and shook his head.

"I tried to get them to change coordinates, but I reacted too slow, I was too late." He sighed. "It's my fault they died."

"No, it's not, they were casualties of war and will be honored as such for the rest of time. You can't blame yourself for that," Isis said. Casper looked up at her and smiled.

"So why aren't you in uniform? All other military personnel here are," he asked.

"Uh oh am I in trouble?" Isis asked.

"No, I won't tell." Casper smiled. Isis nodded and leaned in close to him.

"Truth is I hate the dress uniform, it's much easier to be a civilian," she admitted. "It's like wearing a body cast." Casper laughed out loud.

"God, I wish I had that freedom, unfortunately I'm a prince and that includes everything that goes with it," he replied. Somehow Isis was a refreshing face, unlike the stuffy ones he had been forced to deal with all night. Isis looked around them and then over to his family.

"Can you get away for a few minutes?" she whispered. "I've got this place that's great for relaxing." The offer was one Casper knew he should refuse, especially coming from a lower-ranking officer who was under his command but still, he wanted a break, he needed a break.

"How far?" he asked.

"Not far, walking distance, meet you at the palace gates in ten minutes." She winked. Then without another word she turned on her heels and headed down the stairs. Casper was left in a tizzy as to what exactly had just happened. Had Ensign Soul just hit on him? Or was she just being nice and saw that he needed a break? In any case he was up for some fun, so he decided he would try and make his exit as quickly and quietly as possible.

He slowly turned and started off down one of the palace hallways to get changed. Due to his parents' popularity and his older brother's pretty face, no one noticed Casper's exit.

He made it to his room and changed as quickly as possible and was headed to the secret exit out of the castle from his room when suddenly there was a knock at the door. Casper sighed and went over to the door and opened it only slightly. Harper stood on the other side of the door with Maverick.

"Hey there you are, we thought we'd lost you." Harper smiled.

"Yeah, hey imagine that, uh…is there something you two needed?" he asked. Harper looked at Maverick and then back to Casper.

"Not really. Your brother wanted to go out into town and get a drink, we were wondering if you wanted to come?" Harper asked.

"Uh no, I'm turning in early, goodnight," Casper said. Before they could reply he closed the door and initiated the lock, then he slipped out the back entrance and made for the palace gates.

When he got there Isis was nowhere in sight. He looked around but saw no one. He sighed, he knew the offer from such a pretty girl was too good to be true. Casper sighed and turned back to the palace when all of a sudden he heard a dull whir behind him.

"I know I was late, but I didn't think I was that late," Isis said. Casper turned and saw Isis standing on a hovering platform a foot off the ground. She leaned on the control arch smiling at him. She too had changed into a tank top and jeans.

"You're just on time." He smiled.

"Hop aboard." She smiled. He did so but was a little unsteady, so Isis grabbed his hands and wrapped them around her waist. "Hold on tight, I like speed," she said. Before Casper could reply they zoomed off into the night air.

CHAPTER TWO

An hour later Casper stood barefoot on the beautiful blue sand of the Tamaris Beach looking out onto one of the planet's oceans. The blue sand was a natural effect because of certain minerals derived from the ground. That beautiful color along with the three moons of Hearth Condes just over the horizon was enough to take his breath away. It was such a peaceful image, one that Casper didn't think was still possible of being in existence.

"Gorgeous isn't it?" Isis asked. Casper barely managed to nod in agreement.

"I feel…small, I've never felt like this before," he said.

"It feels good sometimes," Isis said. Casper looked at her, catching her pretty soft-skinned face in the moonlight. She was pretty, stunning actually, and whether it was the moon lighting or the sound of the waves sloshing onto the beach, something was drawing him to her.

He sat down on the beach and Isis sat down beside him and for many minutes they didn't speak at all. Casper was finally able to just sit and think about how simple life could be for once. It was rejuvenating and felt amazing…of course there was something else that was nagging at him. He turned and looked at Isis who sat eyes closed, face up toward the moons. Not quite sure what he was doing or why, Casper took Isis's hand gently causing her to look at him.

"Thank you for this," he said. She smiled warmly at him and blushed slightly.

"Can I be honest with you, sir?" she asked.

"As long as we aren't in uniform, stop calling me sir, it's Casper," he replied. Isis smiled and took his hand, her face was going flush with embarrassment.

"The truth is...Casper...I've had an enormous crush on you since I started working on your ship and found out what you did to save my life." Isis smiled.

"Ah I didn't save your life, I was lying in the infirmary going over a list, the decision of who came over to help was between my engineer and yours," he replied.

"Still...I understand if you don't want to see me anymore I mean...I am being kind of forward and you are my superior officer and the Prince of Hearth Condes. God I've made a fool out of myself." Isis smiled weakly. She pulled her hand out of Casper's and went to move away, but he wouldn't let her. He held both her hands so she couldn't even pull away from him.

"I don't know what it is, but this is the first time I've felt loved in years," Casper said. Without another word he leaned in and kissed her, it felt right and good. When they finally pulled away Isis' blue eyes looked deep into his brown ones with a look of compassion he thought he'd never see toward himself ever again. "Screw the regs, I'm a prince, I'll date whoever I want." Casper smiled. Isis' face lit up, and she wrapped her arms around him. Together they lay on the sand and looked up at the stars, arm in arm with Isis' head on his chest they simply listened to each other breathe. It was a perfect moment, a perfect night, there was nothing that could possibly ruin this for him...

Suddenly all hell broke loose, flashing lights, loud sirens and the rush of hover vehicles. Then came the voices over loudspeakers.

"Prince Casper, are you alright? Do you need assistance?" a voice bellowed.

"Aw fuck me…" Casper sighed. He rolled onto his stomach and looked up at the roadway and saw what appeared to be half the royal guard dismounting their vehicles.

"Whoa, that's what happens when you sneak out?" Isis asked. Casper felt awful, he could only imagine what she was thinking about him at the moment. More still he was embarrassed but knew no moment as perfect as the one he had just experienced could ever last. He stood up and dusted off the sand of his clothing and helped Isis to her feet.

"I'm sorry about this, Isis, can you get home okay?" he asked.

"I can, are you going to be okay?" she asked.

"I'll survive, I'm really sorry about this Isis, I…I think this is goodbye," Casper said. Isis looked shocked and confused.

"W…what? Why?" she asked. He took her hand and kissed it again.

"I don't want you to lose any of the spirit I see in you…that will happen if I suck you into this life. I, I'm sorry Isis I…really I don't know what else to say." He sighed. Isis's eyes filled with tears, and she pulled her hand away.

"I can't believe you're making this choice for me," she said.

"It's not a choice, Isis. I'm sorry but I'm doing this for you," Casper tried. He wanted her to understand that he was saving her from a life he hated, from a life he wished on no person especially one he had feelings for.

"For me? For me? You aren't doing anything for me, Casper, you…you're just being selfish! I'm sorry I'm not good enough for you!" she yelled. In one swift movement she brought her hand around hard and struck Casper right across the face and then jumped on her board and drove off.

Casper was still rubbing his cheek when Harper followed by some of the royal guard came up to him.

"Hey, Casper, what happened? Are you alright?" Harper asked. Casper looked in the direction that Isis had disappeared off into, his heart feeling the loss but at the same time feeling anger.

"I'm fine damn it! Why does everyone keep asking me that??

Can't you all just leave me alone for once? All I want is one god damn second to myself!" Casper exclaimed. He stomped off toward the cars and got in one of them and slammed the door, if he was being forced back to the palace he'd at least choose how he'd go back.

The moment Casper was back at the palace he was cornered in one of the many palace rooms by his family and Harper. His father had started with security protocols and his brother had helped, then his mother came along with the worry that they supposedly felt by finding out he was gone. Last but not least was his brother, yet again stressing the importance of not doing anything that could shed bad light on the family name. That last part had caused Casper to cover his face in exasperation.

"Cass, are you even listening to anything we've said?" Maverick asked. "It's important that you be protected at all times. Not everyone around here is friendly toward our family."

"Uh huh," Casper replied.

"You should listen to your brother, Casper, it's a dangerous world," Anthony said.

"Okay."

"We worry about you, Casper, and we scold you because..." before Patricia could say anymore Casper stood threateningly and glared at them all.

"Don't even say it, Mother, don't you dare say it and expect me to swallow it!" he exclaimed. "This family has seen me as an outcast since day one! None of you can actually pretend that my going out on my own for a few hours means anything to you. You three are the politicians and I'm the soldier. I can protect myself because it's all I know how to do. I shut harmful people out and that is what I have done with you three. You three don't know what reality is because you're too busy kissing everyone's ass! Screw this family, as soon as the ships are ready I'll take off again with my real family..." Casper shoved past them all and headed to the door. When he reached the door handle he stopped and looked at his family one more time. "And next time don't bother seeing me off, I'd rather you not care than fake it," he said. Then he disappeared out into the hallway and ran all the way back to his room.

Once inside he locked the door and headed out onto his deck. He could still see the three moons shining down on the city and could still picture Isis's sweet face. The taste of her fruity lip gloss was still in his mouth and her soft skin on his hands. In one single moment she had made him feel so alive and ingrained that feeling on his mind. He wish she was there now. What he said was stupid, he shouldn't have shut her out like he did. The problem was he had been so engrossed in self-pity that he didn't even give her opinion a second thought. Now he had lost possibly the only woman who could help him feel again.

As his mind started to shut down with exhaustion and loneliness he turned around and decided that the only thing to do now was go to bed. Just as he was about to shut the door to the balcony he heard a metal on marble sound. He spun around just in time to see a grappling hook set roots on the railing. Curious he went over to the edge and looked down. A dark figure was climbing up the rope very quickly. A panic set into his mind and he went to call security but was stopped when he heard his name being called. He spun around and the dark figure came into the light of his bedroom.

"Isis???" Casper exclaimed. She looked like she had been crying quite hard, her eyes were red and her face flush.

"Casper, I refuse to accept you felt nothing on the beach tonight," she said. "You said you have never felt like that before! You said it was the first time you felt loved in years!" she said. Casper didn't need to think about it, he didn't even need to consider it. He hadn't felt like that in years, the beach had been special. Having her go to such lengths could only strengthen the fact that they were meant for each other.

His entire body was overflowing with emotions at the moment, and he was almost unable to move.

"Casper please…say something," Isis whispered. Casper didn't breathe a word. He walked over to Isis, put his hand around the back of her head and pulled her into a deep kiss. She still tasted like the fruity lip gloss she had on and her skin was as smooth as silk. He pulled her entire body into his and for some reason felt the need to be as close to her as possible. She made him *feel* which was something he needed so much at that moment.

They separated but only by mere centimeters, as he stared into her eyes he could still feel her heavy breathing from the long kiss they had just shared.

"I need you so much right now," he whispered to her.

"I'm all yours," she said back. No more words were spoken as they leaned into each other again and started to kiss. Casper wasted no time sweeping Isis off her feet and carrying her over to the bed. For the first time in a long time Casper was feeling a real relationship with another human being, and as Isis slipped off her tank top, it was a relationship with a *fine-looking* human being!

The next morning when Casper woke up he smiled; a slender hand lay across his chest and the night came back to him. His smile got even bigger when he realized he felt like he was on top of the world at the moment. His smile got so big he almost let a laugh escape his lips.

"You're looking happy this morning." Casper looked beside him and saw Isis was half awake nuzzling her head into his chest.

"It's because I have you here with me," he said. Just then there was a noise outside Casper's room. It was still too early for any of the staff to be up yet and the noise just didn't sound right.

"I heard it too," Isis said. He looked at her again and saw she was wide awake now and looking at the door.

"Stay here, I'll check it out," he said. He got out of bed quietly and pulled on a pair of boxers. Then he reached into his desk drawer where he kept his weapon. It was a simple crystal combat blade that when switched on conducted 500 volts of raw electricity. The knife had done a lot of damage during Casper's several years of combat and he thought of it as an extension of his arm.

Moving into combat mode Casper slipped out of his room like a ghost and instantly saw a tipped-over planter in the hallway. His instincts had been right, something was wrong. This instinct brought him to one other concern, Maverick's room was just down the hall from his own. It was a big house and his mother and father's room was far enough away that at the moment his main concern was his brother.

Casper crept along to his brother's door and found that it was open. He knew not to just go bursting in. He got as close as he could to the wall and peered around the door frame and gasped silently. A man with a mask on had Maverick at gunpoint and was putting binders on his hands and feet. A binder was a small device that when switched on paralyzed seven inches above and below wherever placed on the skin.

The look on Maverick's face was that of sheer terror, but at the same time utter defiance. Casper was glad his brother was still being defiant if only with his eyes. What seemed to be going on was the man was binding Maverick in order to take him away; if the attacker had wanted Maverick dead he probably would have done so already.

Once bound the man yanked Maverick to his feet and started to drag him to the balcony. Now that the man's back was turned to the door Casper saw his chance and moved in to save his brother. He moved swiftly and quietly. Maverick saw him and his eyes went huge. Casper switched on his blade and lunged, unfortunately for him when the blade switched on it made a buzz noise. It was a brief short noise, but it was enough to alert the assailant.

The man tossed Maverick to the floor and spun around just in time to catch Casper's wrist. The man turned out to be much, *much* stronger than Casper had anticipated as his grip on Casper's wrist was so strong it was cutting off the circulation.

"You think your little prince weapon can hurt me?" the man hissed

"Fuck you, I'm not a prince, I'm a soldier," Casper said, gritting his teeth against the pain. Under the mask, Casper saw a wicked smile as it was clear the assailant was slowly winning the physical battle. Casper knew this was going to have to come back to a battle of wits. The idea came to him to start acting as if he was really struggling but really drawing the man closer to the balcony.

"Right, you're the fighter in the family, all guns and no brains, you'll suffer for that," the man said.

"Will I?" Casper smiled. He had done it, he had caught the man in a trap. They were right at the railing of the balcony. With a swift kick in the shins and a punch in the stomach he pushed the man over the edge. Immediately he turned to free his brother only to find Isis was doing it for him. He was about to ask if Maverick was alright when his brother looked up and went pale.

"Cass, LOOK OUT!!!" Casper spun around just in time to see a hand grab his shirt to fling him over the balcony. Luckily Casper grabbed onto the man and they both went over the edge to the sound of Isis's shrill scream. He wildly grabbed for the balcony and managed to get a firm grip on the railing. The assailant, however, also had a strong grip on his leg. Casper looked around to see where his knife had landed but found it nowhere. It was soon located, however, when a sharp pain rode up his shin muscle in to his brain, and it hadn't even been switched on. Casper looked down after howling in pain and saw the attacker smile with his finger on the button. Just at that moment, Maverick and Isis appeared over the railing and reached down to help Casper up but he stopped them.

"NO! Don't touch me you'll get shocked!" he pained.

"Cass, we can't leave you hanging!" Maverick exclaimed. His brother reached over to help pull him up and Casper knew he had to make a choice. The fall was three stories into the rocky waters below but at this point, he didn't want to run the risk of hurting his brother or Isis. He looked up at the two and smiled.

"See you on the flip side," he said. Then he let go of the railing. A moment into the drop a surge of electricity shot through him blinding him in pain and rendering him helpless to swim to the surface when he splashed into the water.

Underwater and semi-conscious Casper was only semi-aware of what was going on, but he could hear muffled noises. There was what he thought was a splash beside him and he figured it was the assailant swimming to shore. His body still reeling from the shock and the stab wound to his already limp burdened leg, he accepted his fate and things started to go dark.

Just when he thought it was the end he felt two strong arms wrap around him and pull him to the surface. The delightful air was a blessing in his lungs as he coughed out the salty waters that had been filling them.

"Hang on, Cass, I got you," Maverick breathed. Casper pieced together that his brother must have jumped into the water after him saving him from a most certain death.

Maverick pulled Casper up on shore where several of the royal guards and staff awaited with blankets to wrap around him. The palace doctor was also on hand to mend his lacerated leg wound. Out of the crowd of people came his parents and Isis and they crowded to his side.

"Oh god, my boys are you alright?" Patricia exclaimed.

"What happened?" Anthony asked.

"Someone came into my room trying to kidnap me and…"

"You just flew off the balcony, sir! That was incredible how you saved your brother like that!" the doctor exclaimed. Casper couldn't believe it. If he had been stable enough to explain what happened he'd punch the doctor right in the face. Maverick was looking like the hero?? What the hell kind of justice was that??

"Oh Maverick you saved him! And after you were attacked," Anthony said. "Well done, son." Casper was looking at them all, the rage building in his mind but the lack of energy stopping him from expressing it.

"Actually, Casper is the hero here, he saved Maverick and risked his life to protect the both of us," Isis said. Casper managed a smile and reached out shakily to take her hand. When she felt his hand she held it tightly and smiled down at him.

"Who are you by the way?" Maverick asked. Isis looked at him and then down to Casper.

"I'm…" she began.

"…girlfriend…" Casper choked out.

"Come, let's get you all inside and warmed up," Patricia said. Somehow Casper had a feeling they had heard nothing Isis had put on the record as protest. So as he was helped into the house he made sure to give Isis an appreciative smile. Almost to say, "thanks for trying."

Two hours later Casper was warm, healed, changed, and sitting down for breakfast with his family and Isis whom his mother had invited to stay. He poked at his food, again finding no great urge to put any of it in his mouth. The coffee that had been set out for him struck him as much more alluring than anything else so he decided to nurse that instead.

"So how did you two meet?" Patricia asked.

"I'm in the service," Isis said vaguely. She knew as much as Casper did his parents wouldn't approve of her much lower rank than his own.

"Ah, good military woman then. It's nice to meet you," Anthony said.

"And you, sir and ma'am, I can't tell you what an honour it is to be sitting at the same table as our Sovereign rulers," Isis smiled. God, she was gorgeous., Casper couldn't stop thinking about the night before that they had spent together.

"Cass, you going to eat or suck on that coffee until lunch?" Maverick asked. Suddenly everyone's attention was focused on him and he felt slightly awkward.

"Are you okay, Casper?" Patricia asked.

"YES! Fuck, stop asking me that!" Casper snapped. Then he realized he was being too harsh and sighed. "I apologize, I'm just rather concerned as to why you all seem to be taking that tack this morning, so lightly." It was then he noticed his family members were all looking at each other nervously, as if they had something they were hiding from him. "Holy hell," Casper exclaimed slowly as the realization hit him. "This has happened before hasn't it?" Again his family was silent and looked away from him. It was true! Casper was shocked and stunned, his family was being attacked by fundamentalists and hadn't bothered to tell him! Immediately Casper jumped to his feet sending his chair flying backward despite the pain in his tender leg.

"Easy, Cass, we didn't want to tell you because we know you've had to deal with a lot recently," Maverick said.

"We were so worried about you that we didn't want to distract you from coming home safely," Patricia said.

"No, no, don't try and spin it like that," Casper shot back. "How could it possibly be a good idea *not* to tell me my family has been attacked time and time again!?!"

"You're exaggerating, Casper, it hasn't been like that at all," Anthony said.

"OH REALLY??? Tell me *Dad* how many times has it happened that's made you accustomed to attacks?" Casper shot back. His father looked away not wanting to answer the question truthfully but obviously not wanting to lie to his son.

"Four times, not including today," Maverick sighed. Casper went wide-eyed with disbelief and disgust.

"What kind of security to you have watching this place? CHILDREN WITH POINTY STICKS??" he yelled. Beside him Isis took his wrist and tried to get him to sit back down and relax.

"The palace security is *fine*, Casper, those damn fundamentalists manage to get around our security ever time we change it. We've developed a solid system that…" Casper didn't even let his brother finish his sentence.

"OBVIOUSLY not good enough! A deaf, dumb, blind monkey could do better! This is ridiculous, give me two days of control of the security and I'll have this place tighter than a fortress. Anyone tries to get over the walls will be dealt with as I see fit…we can set an example to the rest of the maniacs out there by public execution," Casper said. Once he finished his sentence he realized he wasn't talking to other soldiers, he was talking to his family and people who have never seen more then a trickle of blood in their entire lives. His mother looked horrified, his brother and father shocked that such violence had just come from their little prince. Isis, however, looked fine but continued to urge him to sit down.

"Somehow I think that's a little drastic, and I think I'm taking care of homeland security well enough, Casper. You stick to your ships," Maverick said. Once again, Casper felt left out and hurt. His family didn't want him to interfere with their business of politics. They wanted him to get back on his ship and disappear into space, to fight a dying war against other human beings who just didn't see where his people were coming from. Religion and power, it was the same in space as it was on Hearth Condes.

Casper had exhausted all his willpower trying to be accepted by his family, he just didn't have the energy to bother anymore. He turned away from the table without a word and headed for the doorway.

"Son, don't walk away in the middle of a conversation," Anthony called. Casper stopped but didn't turn around.

"Why? I'm not a part of this family anyway, what does it matter if I go or stay?" he asked.

"Where has this hostility come from, Casper? We love you, it's never been any different," Patricia said.

"That's just it, *we* love, as in this family loves me even though I'm not really a part of it," Casper said.

"That's a lie and you know it," Maverick snapped. Casper turned to see his brother was now standing threateningly and pointing to the table. "Sit back down, we're going to talk about this right now."

"Go to hell, Mav," Casper hissed. He headed for the door again and was almost out when a strong arm on his spun him around.

"Things aren't great right now, and I'm tired of your self-pity mission!" Maverick exclaimed.

"I'm giving you to the count of five to take your hands off me," Casper came back.

"Oh and what are you going to do? Put *me* up for public execution you psychopath?" Maverick yelled. By now both men were standing off against the other ignoring the rest of the family.

"Calm down boys, there's no need for this," Anthony said calmly. However, Casper nor Maverick would have any of it.

"Public execution is what you deserve, pretty boy! All you ever do is sit on your ass and talk! I'd like to see you in a pressure suit trying to get the enemy off the hull of your ship before he sets off a mine!" Casper said. Maverick threw his arms in the air dramatically and laughed sarcastically.

"Oh the truth comes out!" he exclaimed. "Now I know where the attitude is coming from! It's because you think you're better then us! Just because you can kick ass and take numbers doesn't mean you're anything more then a pathetic wastrel!"

"Ooh big word! Did you have to look that up?"

"At least I spend more time reading than I do planning public executions!"

"Yeah and now I'm planning one more—yours!!!" That was it, Casper wasn't sure who snapped first but didn't care. Maverick took the first swing, but then it was Casper who reacted like a trained soldier getting low, tackling Maverick, literally lifting the man off his feet sending them both flying into the breakfast table. Food and drink went flying in all directions and his parents along with Isis were forced to get out of the way.

Casper went into a blind rage that he was accustomed to doing when fighting hand to hand with the enemy; an enemy who at this point, was his older brother.

"You've gotten stronger you little shit," Maverick groaned angrily.

"Because I've been waiting to do this for a long time…" with that Casper struck his brother right in the face knocking Maverick flat out on the broken table. His brother shook it off and got up to lunge at him again, but Casper was already shifting into his next move. Before his brother could touch him, Casper stuck out his hand grabbing Maverick by the throat and clothes-lining him to the ground. At which point Casper used his other hand as back up and proceeded to strangle Maverick.

Pinning his brother to the ground making sure there was no chance of escape, he continued to struggle with him, searching with his eyes for some sort of weapon. His brother was right, he had gotten stronger and was effortlessly winning the battle.

Something happened to Casper at that moment. As the rage boiled inside him, the calls of his family suddenly ceased and Casper found himself back on his ship, *The Specter*. He was running down the hall trying to pull on his uniform as the ship rocked violently back and forth. Casper knew what was happening, they were being attacked from the outside! The fundamentalists had planted mines on the damn flagship of the squadron!

Casper had been sleeping when the first mine exploded, there was no telling how many there were nor where they were. That was the problem with the mines that could be planted directly onto the hull of the ship. Finally Casper reached the bridge and saw the night crew looking very frazzled.

"Report!!" he yelled.

"They're all over the hull!! God there must be...hundreds!!" Harper exclaimed in disbelief.

"How the fuck did they get so many without us knowing??" Casper cried out.

"I don't know! I DON'T KNOW!!" Harper shot back. It was clear the poor weaponry officer had his hands full at the moment and had no time to deal with the why but rather the how to stop it. Another explosion rocked the ship sending everyone in every which direction.

"Son of a bitch, where are they? SOMEONE FUCKING FIND THEM!!!" he yelled.

"Sir, we've got a hull breech in the cargo hold! They're boarding us, sir!" Freddy exclaimed. Casper looked at him incredulously.

"While the mines are still exploding? Are they suicidal?" he asked no one in particular. He turned back to Harper and narrowed his eyes. "Kill them, Harper, every last one of them and if they surrender...kill them anyway."

"Aye, sir," Harper smiled. He pulled out his side arm and raced to the corridor. Casper jumped into his chair and looked at his panel; he could see the squadron had drifted into an ambush.

"Sir, the mines...they're going off in succession," Linda said from her console.

"So what can we expect?" Casper asked.

"Judging by this, sir, they've started at the back and then front and then back again, so the next one should be..." Linda never got to finish. A huge explosion rocked the bridge of the ship, Casper who had only been sitting on the edge of his seat was thrown several meters into a nearby console. Sparks and glass flew everywhere as he collided with the panel. He felt a rush of electricity and then nothing but darkness.

Casper twitched then shot straight up and looked around him breathing heavily. He was back in the palace, but he was no longer in the breakfast room. He sat in his bed with the sheets placed over him. He looked around him and then to his body that was saturated with his own sweat.

Just then his room door opened and Patricia walked in with a damp cloth and a glass of water. When she saw her son was awake she smiled with relief.

"I swear you boys give me nothing but gray hairs," she joked. Casper only smiled weakly as his mother made him lie back down so she could put the cold cloth on his head.

"What happened?" He asked. Patricia frowned as she dabbed his forehead lightly.

"I'm not quite sure, no one is really, one moment you're raising a shard of glass to your brother's head and the next…you just kind of…froze," she replied.

"Froze?" Casper repeated. His mother nodded.

"That's the only way to explain it really, you just stopped where you were and had this very vacant look in your eye. Maverick simply pushed you away and tried to snap you out of it, but then your eyes rolled back in your head and you passed out," she said. Casper sighed.

"How long was I out?" he asked.

"It's only been a half hour," she said. "But you had me so worried, so scared." Again Casper closed his eyes and took a deep breath to try and grasp what had just happened to him. He knew of people who had suffered flashbacks triggered by a sudden onslaught of rage or sadness but never knew how powerful they could actually be.

"I think I need to leave the palace," Casper concluded. His mother looked at him confused.

"What? Why?" she asked.

"Because Mother…Mom, I just…I don't think I can be around you guys anymore. I'm too much of a risk, I nearly killed Maverick today and had no qualms in doing so. Until now that is, but still, I think it's better for us all if I leave." He sighed.

"Running from your problems won't fix them, Casper honey. You need to work things out with your brother, father, and me." Patricia smiled gently. Casper looked up at her and all at once wished he was six years old again; no worries, no duties, just a mother and son. But it wasn't that simple now, and it would never be like that again. Casper had to make a choice and he made it already.

"I'm sorry, I have to go," he replied. "There's a service run to the outer moon of Hearth, they need a security detail to escort them. I was going to send one of the other ships, but I think I'll take the *Specter* instead. It'll be a three-week trip because the transport vessel doesn't have light speed capabilities, so by the time I get back the rest of my squadron will be ready to head back to the Achilles Quadrant to join the guys from Marquise system and patrol the border." Patricia's gentle smile faltered and she looked at her frail hands.

"I'm not a soldier like you and your father, you know that." She sighed.

"I know, but you're still strong, you don't need me around, you've got Maverick," Casper replied. He could see the emotion starting to show on his mother's face, she could have a poker face to fool the devil if she wanted but never would she hide from her own sons.

"One out of two isn't good enough," she whispered. "I love you, Casper, I don't want you to go again so soon. I know it's your job but please, I need you here for at least a year's time."

"I can't do that," Casper said bluntly. It was true, he would have to take the Squadron out again and whether that was in four weeks time or tomorrow it had to be soon. The Marquise humans were good soldiers, but when it came to attention spans they lost theirs very quickly and had the tendency to wander back into old formations or positions that were well known by the enemy.

Patricia turned away from Casper and his heart broke as tears began to slide down his mother's face. He gently took her hand and put his other to the side of her face turning her to look at him.

"It's what I was born to do, Mom. I'm the soldier, Maverick's the politician. We both have duties to this planet and to humanity, unfortunately mine are away from home," he explained.

"But you don't have to go so soon!" his mother wept. "You don't need to go on this supply run, nor do you need to leave once the ships are ready to go! I want you here, son, I want you safe in my arms like when you were a baby!" Casper smiled gently and brought his mother into his arms hugging her tightly so as to soothe her.

"I know, I'm sorry it just has to be like this, Mom. I can't stay here and run the risk of attacking Maverick or you or dad. I won't do that to my family, and I won't do that to myself." He sighed. His mother clung to him much as he imagined he would have as a small boy for support.

"No, please don't go, I beg you please! I don't want to lose my son to those maniacs!" she cried. Casper took a deep breath and could see he wasn't getting through to her at all. He held her out at arms' length so as to look her in the eye.

"It will be alright, I have many good men and women under my service, you met one of them in Isis. I'll come back to you, I promise," he said soothingly. Still his mother didn't seem any less distraught.

"You don't know how many times you went away or Maverick was entangled in a political mess or your lives were put under the microscope that I wished you hadn't been born into this life. I always wanted you two to have a normal childhood like in the city where the boys and girls would go to school and laugh and play. Then I'd see you two with your private tutors because it was too dangerous to leave the palace gates, and I'd feel responsible that I brought you into this world and yet was letting you see none of it. Sometimes I wished…I wish things were different for you boys. I'm sorry you couldn't have a normal childhood, and I'm sorry for what you're forced to endure now." Patricia sniffed. Her tears had stopped and she had regained some of her composure, while Casper had lost some of his. He was rather startled and caught off guard by the admonition his mother had just put before him.

"Don't blame yourself for this life, Mom, no regrets because it's not your fault. We can't choose the lives we are born into. Maverick and I have turned out fine, save a few brawls at the breakfast table," Casper joked lightly. His mother let out a tired laugh and shook her head. "I understand what you are saying, and I understand how much you want me to stay, how much *I* want to stay for that matter and talk about this more with dad and Mav."

"So you'll stay? Send someone else on the service trip?" Patricia asked hopefully. Her eyes were pleading with him, the way she held his hands in hers as if hoping it would force him to stay. Alas Casper turned away from her gently hopeful eyes and placed her hands back in her own lap.

"Again, I'm sorry, Mom, but I have to, believe me going is for the best." He sighed. With that he stood up and left the room. As he did he could hear his mother weeping into his pillow and had to use every fiber of his will power not to go back to her. Casper knew that if he turned back and rejoined her, he would definitely crack and promise to stay longer. He had barely made it out of the room that first time let alone a second. It was a tough decision, but he knew his family would be fine without him for almost another year. The Hawks were strong resilient people who never stepped down from a challenge nor shied from a problem.

Things would heal with time, he was sure of it, but it was too soon. Too soon to start talking about feelings when they were still raw from war, and too soon to talk of war when it was still a subject of raw emotions. He'd be back as he had promised, but that wouldn't be anytime soon.

"And a promise is a promise, Mom, you just have to stay strong until then," Casper said to himself, wiping away a single tear of his breaking heart.

He had just done speaking to the supply ship captain and was walking along the interior docking port when quickly moving footsteps caught his attention behind him. Casper slowed and turned only to have Harper, Freddy, and Linda plow right into him.

"Where the hell do you think *you're* going?" Harper asked.

"I was about to ask you the same question, what are you guys doing here?" Casper asked.

"We're your crew, sir, we go where you go," Linda replied. Casper smiled at the dedication of his soldiers but shook his head.

"This isn't a military op, it's a simple supply run. I'm taking a ghost crew on the *Specter*, people who I think need a little more time at their stations before we go operational again. Guys, I'll be back in three weeks to get the squadron ready to get on her way again," Casper said.

"I think we want to know why you're going in the first place." Casper turned and behind him Commander Danielle Tyson was strolling up to the group.

"What is this a freaking intervention?" Casper asked.

"No, it's a group of friends," Danielle said. She nodded hello to the others and then turned back to Casper. Danielle was an amazing leader, sometimes better than Casper was himself. The woman stood a towering six-foot-five but was built like a Greek goddess. Her feminine stature was no way an indication of what she was capable of. Danielle's mind was sharp as a tack, she moved her tall frame like it was nothing at all in a split second if the situation required.

She was literally the ultimate woman, for any adventure-seeking man, but to Casper she was the sister he never had. That's why he had put the *Spartan* at his side in nearly every formation. Split-second leadership decisions were Danielle's forte. This had been proven quite well when the *Specter* had been ambushed inside and out and the bridge crew was almost entirely incapacitated.

When Casper awoke in the infirmary he remembered Danielle standing over him with a smile. She explained that she had gotten the squadron to form a wall with the *Specter* on the inside. Then each ship had sent an overwhelming force of ten men each. Through sheer power the ambush had ceased because the enemy had so suddenly been out numbered and outgunned.

"Then as my friends, mind your P's and Q's," Casper said.

"Captain, I thought the *Spartan* was going on this run, the workups been done and she's ready to go right now. You'd still have to prep the *Specter* and call in her crew," Danielle said.

"Which is what I'll do, stand down the *Spartan* commander, she's not needed today," Casper said. His friends didn't looked convinced in the slightest and looked rather annoyed.

"Then the three of us are going as well," Freddy said. But Casper was already shaking his head denying the request.

"No way, I want inexperienced crew so they can get experience, there's no point in having good men on a plain mission like this," Casper said.

"Okay…cause that explains why *you're* going," Harper chided. Casper opened his mouth to reply but suddenly realized he'd been out played at his own game. He snarled and looked at his hands trying to come up with a response.

"Speechless," Linda smiled. "I think you got him, sir." And he did, Harper looked quite pleased with himself. Casper shook his head finally and took a deep breath.

"Look, I need to do this alone with people I don't know. I guess…I need to get away for a bit guys, that's really all I'm saying," he said truthfully.

"It's kind of soon isn't it? I mean, what does your family think?" Freddy asked.

"They're the reason I need to get away for a bit. I nearly killed Maverick the other day without a second thought. It's for everyone's good," Casper replied. Then he looked his friends in the eyes so they could see how tired he was. "I'm not going to order you to stay because we are all friends, but I'd really like to take this one without you so I can get my head together." There was a moment of silence as his words were pondered by the whole group. Then Harper was the first one to sigh and look back up at him.

"I'll stand down if that's what you want," he said.

"Myself as well," Linda replied.

"Ditto," Freddy added. Which left Danielle's decision and really the one that mattered almost as much as Harper's did. She looked up at him and shook her head.

"Fine," she sighed. "But steal the *Spartan*'s thunder like that again and I'll keehaul you off the bow," she joked. Casper smiled as the others laughed.

"Come on, lunch is on me," he said. The group smiled and they all started toward the lift.

CHAPTER THREE

The next morning Casper was back on the bridge of his ship waiting for the word to take off alongside the transport vessel. He hadn't seen his brother at all the night before, which made sense after what Casper had done to him. Casper had slightly regretted not saying goodbye to Maverick but shoved it to the back of his mind. His mother had begged him right up until he boarded his ship to stay, but finally wished him a safe journey when she accepted the fact that he was not staying. His father had looked at him and said he understood what he was doing and why, but then added simply that it wasn't the right thing to do.

Casper wasn't quite sure what he had meant by that but shrugged it off and bid his family adieu.

"Sir, we're getting departing coordinates from command central," said the crewman at the com panel where Linda usually stayed.

"Send the coordinates to Ensign Orion and open a channel to the transport," Casper ordered. Moments later the link was established.

"I'm honored to have you with us, sir," said the captain of the transport.

"Just doing my duty, Captain." Casper smiled. "You lead, I

follow?" he offered. The captain smiled over the view screen and nodded.

"Try and keep up," he joked. Casper laughed and nodded, with that they terminated the link and the ship shuddered to life as she lifted from the platform behind the transport.

"Here we go, ladies and gents," Casper said to no one in particular. He was keeping the mood light but part of him was still hurting from leaving his family like he did. They had wanted him to stay and talk so badly, but he wasn't ready for that; they'd have to wait.

A few hours after they left the planet Casper stood up from his chair to hand the bridge over to the next shift. He was too tired to eat lunch, so he figured he would just head to his quarters and rest a little.

However, when he reached his quarters and found his door unlocked Casper was suddenly wide awake. He slowly entered his room looking around cautiously, a slight cough from his desk caught his attention and slowly he approached the back of the chair. The man sitting there was facing away from him but clearly had made himself comfortable. Casper was about to spin the chair around when the man spun the chair around himself and stood.

"YAAAAAAAAAAAAAAAAAAAAAAAAAAAAAARGH!!!" Casper exclaimed. The man had scared the crap out of him and he stumbled backward slightly, then he saw who it was. "MAVERICK??? What are you DOING here???" His brother walked around the desk and sauntered over to one of the windows to watch the stars.

"I came to a decision about you, Cass," he said.

"That being?" Casper asked. His heart was still slowing itself down from the jolt it just received.

"I let you go last time, I won't do it again," he replied. Casper was confused.

"What do you mean?" he asked. Maverick sighed and turned to look at him.

"I mean you didn't have to go alone to the Achilles quadrant. Dad asked me if I wanted to go as well, to see if I like the service more than politics. I said no, I was too afraid, but I didn't tell him that. Then you went and I heard of the things that were happening to you and I regretted that choice. Now you come back and you've changed so much…I don't want you to leave again and come back someone I don't even recognize because of what you've gone through. When we fought yesterday I said that you thought you were better than us…truth was it was my own jealousy. I wish I could see the things you've seen, be a part of the life you've lived so as to better understand but…I'm just not as strong a man as you are," Maverick explained.

"Wow," Casper breathed. Truly he had no idea what to say at that point. His brother just completely blew him away. For years Casper had been jealous that his older brother always had the lucky breaks, and now it seemed Maverick was just as jealous of him! "I mean…wow," Casper said again. "I really have no idea what to say." Maverick shrugged and looked at the stars again.

"About a month after you left I realized how I felt and I wanted to tell you in a letter, but every time I started a letter it would come out wrong. I just couldn't get out how I really felt, then Mom told me last night you were planning on leaving again and…I knew I had to tell you the truth. Every time you get on a ship I was always afraid I was going to end up an only child. If I could have half the amount of courage you do…" Maverick trailed off. Casper still couldn't find his voice, what his brother was saying was just too shocking for him to even comprehend.

"I'm a big fat fake, Cass, all talk and no walk. I'm afraid to leave the palace without an armed guard, and then there's you—you took off the other night with a woman you barely knew to a place you didn't know and thought nothing of it. I could never do that," Maverick added. Finally Casper found his voice and appreciated Maverick much more than he ever had before.

"Yet here you are, you snuck aboard a military vessel, probably didn't tell anyone and risked total and utter rejection faced by a three week voyage completely on your own with out a mouse to talk to," he replied. Maverick turned to face him with a confused look on his face which slowly cleared into a smile.

"I did, didn't I?" He smiled. Casper nodded with a smile and then thought of something.

"Hey yeah, that's right…this *is* a military vessel, you need a pass card to get on this ship even if you are you! How did you…" Casper trailed off. There was only one person that could have possibly aided Maverick in his stunt and if Maverick was on board it undoubtedly meant *he* was on board as well. Casper sighed and turned around looking at his supposedly empty room.

"The jig is up, Harper. I know you're in here, you're the only one with the code to hack the lock on my door," he sighed. After a brief pause Casper's closet door opened and Harper stepped out rather embarrassed.

"I was hoping you wouldn't figure it out," he mumbled. Casper shook his head,

"You don't really expect me to believe that do you?" Harper pursed his lips and then smiled mischievously.

"Not really, I was already making plans to sneak aboard when your brother approached me for help. Don't worry the others aren't here, I convinced them you'd be more willing to accept just one of us rather than all of us." He smiled. Casper laughed and sighed.

"You two are going to be the death of me," he admitted. Maverick and Harper laughed, then Casper turned to Maverick and looked him in the eye. "Actually Mav, I'm really glad you came…you too Harp, it…means a lot to me," he said. Maverick came over to his brother and patted him on the back with a smile.

"Me too…now you can show me how a military ship works," he said.

"Definitely," Casper smiled. Then he turned to Harper. "As long as you're here you can keep an eye on the new guys on the ship, some of them are real rooks." Harper snapped to attention trying to hide his smile.

"Aye, sir," he replied. Harper spun on his heels and made for the door. Casper turned back to Maverick with a smile.

"You want to see what kind of fire power this bad girl has?" he asked. Maverick's face lit up like every boy's face would at the chance to see something really cool that had the capability to blow something up.

"Let's go!" he exclaimed. Casper laughed and turned toward the door. He planned to take Maverick to the engine room and was heading there when they stepped into the lift but things changed in the blink of an eye. Halfway down the corridor the ship rocked violently from side to side.

"What the heck was that??" Maverick demanded. Casper didn't answer, he was used to surprises but not when they happened on a simple supply run.

"Stay on my heels and don't get lost, Mav," Casper ordered. Then he took off toward the bridge to get control of his ship and the situation.

They reached the bridge and found Harper had shoved the poor ensign at the security console out of the way. He looked up when Casper and Maverick entered, the look on his face told it all. Something was wrong, he didn't know what, but he was trying to figure it out, and in the meantime, it appeared as if the situation was desperate.

"A mine?" Casper asked.

"No."

"A ship?"

"No..."

"Then what was it?" Harper looked up, his forehead creased with confusion and concern.

"Nothing, there's nothing on sensors, any of them...it's like...we hit an invisible wall," he replied.

"What about the transport, is she okay?" Casper asked. Harper looked down at his panel and then up again.

"She's stopped on our port, but there appears to be nothing wrong with her. I think she stopped for our benefit," he replied.

"Open a com," Casper ordered. He took his place in his captain's chair and waited for the face of the transport captain to appear. When it did the civilian captain looked concerned.

"You alright? Your ship stopped so suddenly we barely managed to stop without ripping ourselves to pieces," he said.

"We aren't quite sure what happened, captain…" Casper was cut off when Harper cursed absentmindedly.

"Engines are gone…we're sitting ducks." He sighed. Casper nodded keeping his cool and turning back to the captain.

"We can give you a tow if you like, there's a friendly space port a few light years from here…"

"That's very generous of you, sir, but you've done enough by stopping and asking if we need assistance. I'd rather not risk losing a supplier vessel for a bunch of grunts such as ourselves." Casper smiled diplomatically. "No, what I'm going to do is send over a shuttle of my best people, I figure thirty ought to do it. I'd like you to let them take over security and make for your rendezvous for the moon station as quick as you can. The *Specter* will stay put and contact Hearth for some repairs and we'll join you as soon as we can."

"That I can do, Captain Hawk, and again, thank you," the supply captain said. Casper nodded and once the communication was ended he turned to Harper, who looked up at him exasperated.

"No, I'm staying here, I promised your parents I'd protect your ass and that's what I'm going to do. I will gather the thirty people you promised and send them on their way but I'm not going anywhere," he said sternly. Casper could see Harper was standing firm on his position and was unmovable.

"Okay, do it as quick as possible and then get back to the bridge," he replied. Harper nodded then jumped up from his console and disappeared; meanwhile, Casper turned to Ensign Orion who was piloting the ship.

"What's happening, Orion?" he asked calmly.

"I really couldn't tell you, sir, it's almost like we were…hit with an EMP. Systems are failing all over the ship," Orion replied.

"Life support?"

"Still holding strong, sir…it's really the only one," Orion said. Casper cursed under his breath then looked at his own panel to confirm what he was being told and cursed again. Just as he thought things couldn't get any worse, the main lighting failed and the sensor in front of him went blank.

"I take it that's *not* a normal occurrence." Casper had almost forgotten his brother was standing just feet behind him and turned his attention to Maverick.

"No, it's not, someone is messing with my baby and I don't appreciate it," he replied. "You can head back to my room if you want, I'm going to be here a while."

"Actually if it's all the same, I'd like to stay and watch." Maverick shrugged. Despite the situation Casper smiled and nodded to his brother.

"Of course," he said. Then he turned back to Orion who had moved to the security panel to see if there was any hope of seeing what hit them. "What do you have for me, Orion?"

"A blank screen, sir, I..." Orion stopped as some of the stations flickered to life including his. Then suddenly Orion's eyes went huge and his mouth nearly hit the floor as he glared at the panel.

"Ensign? What is it?" Casper asked.

"I...I'm not quite sure, sir it's..." Orion stopped as he looked closer at the panel.

"What, Ensign, it's what?" After a bit of a pause the man was finally able to answer, as he looked up at Casper still wide-eyed.

"Huge, sir...I have no idea what it is but...it's *huge*," he replied. Casper looked at the view screen and saw nothing, then he looked back to Orion and walked over to the station. According to the sensor, there was something incredibly large approaching their aft ship. But there was nothing on the view screen. *Why the hell couldn't they see it?*

"Sir..." the crewman sitting at the com-panel now had her turn to look shocked.

"What is it crewman?" he asked.

"Uh...we're being hailed," she said. Casper didn't think this was abnormal at all, the supply ship was still in front of them and hadn't left yet.

"We already agreed the transport would leave, tell them they can't change their mind now it's too…"

"It's not the transport, sir," she cut off. Now Casper was confused, there weren't any other ships out there, all there was, was…*the ominous gargantuan figure silently sneaking up on them.*

"Put it through," he said. He looked intently at the view screen waiting to see who had just dared stop and sneak up on a military vessel. A moment later a man's face appeared looking quite pleased with himself. Casper didn't recognize the man, but he did the uniform; the man was a high ranking fundamentalist.

"Bernard, you traitorous snake!" Casper was startled by his brother's outburst and turned toward him.

"You know him?" he asked.

"Yes, I'm afraid so." Bernard laughed. "Allow me to introduce myself, Prince Casper, or is it Captain Hawk? My name is Bernard Atkinson, I worked with your brother on many diplomatic missions."

"Secretly destroying most of them, you smug bastard, you should be tried for treason and betrayal to the royal family!" Maverick exclaimed. However, Bernard simply laughed.

"Oh you simple, simple man! Honestly, it took you much too long to figure out what I was doing." He sighed. It was then Casper decided to cut in.

"Hey chuckles, this is my ship, you want to talk, you talk to me not my crew or passengers," he hissed. The man threw his hands in the air and again laughed. Casper would have fun smacking that grin right off his face.

"Quite right, quite right," he replied. "Well I've come to give you an ultimatum."

"What could you possibly offer me that I want? My ship has superior fire power and don't think we don't see you sneaking up behind us," Casper shot back. Still the man remained with a ridiculous smile on his face.

"Good eye, but not good enough, you see, as we've been talking, your crew has failed to see that I've gained the upper hand, dear captain," Bernard smiled. Casper looked down at his sensor to try and see what had changed that wasn't there before but saw nothing different. He looked back up to Bernard and tried to remain calm.

"Okay I give up, what have you done?" he asked.

"Hee...it's not so much *what* I've done but *who* I have done it to." Bernard laughed. Casper was confused, and then he realized something, it had been much too long since he had heard from Harper and the soldiers who had left for the transport.

"What did you do to those men and women I sent to the transport?" he asked.

"Detained their ship you could say...or would you like to see?" Bernard smiled. Suddenly the screen changed to the interior view of the shuttle ship that was moving the soldiers. Casper was horrified as everyone appeared to be unconscious! Even Harper who was sitting in the pilot's chair was slumped to one side. The screen changed back to Bernard's smiling face.

"What did you do to them?" Casper demanded angrily.

"Calm down, they are merely incapacitated, your Lt. Harper put up quite the argument when we detained the ship," Bernard said. "Almost like he had no concern for himself but rather for your own ship, Captain Hawk."

"I'm in no mood for idle chitchat, Atkinson, tell me what you want and let my people go," Casper hissed. Finally the smiling man stopped smiling and looked very, very serious.

"It's simple really, I'll let your crew go, your ship and the transport *if* you give me one thing," Bernard said.

"What?"

"Yourself," Bernard said simply. Casper's mind went into overdrive. He was being taken hostage and he had no choice. "Otherwise I can kill them all right now...starting with Mr. Harper, I believe..."

"No!" Casper exclaimed. He couldn't bear the thought of men and women suffering for his life. "Fine, fine you can have me, but you let everyone else go you promise?"

"My word," Bernard said, raising both hands. Casper sighed heavily and lowered his head in defeat.

"Fine…Orion, lower shields," Casper ordered. However, Orion hesitated, he was too stunned to do anything.

"Casper, no! This is suicide!" Maverick exclaimed.

"I won't let those people die, Maverick. Orion, lower shields," Casper repeated. With a very distraught look Orion did as he was told, moments later Casper felt a tingling sensation as he was removed from the deck of his ship.

When he re-materialized he was in a dark room of sorts, four walls and completely black save the lights under his feet. Suddenly two men rushed into the room and grabbed Casper.

"Hey easy! You're hurting me!" he exclaimed.

"Oh boy…we're going to do *a lot* more than that, Prince." One man laughed. As he did the other man brought his weapon down hard on Casper's skull, instantly knocking him into oblivion.

Over the next couple of hours Casper was forced to endure all kinds of tortures and beatings. Finally just when he knew he was within an inch of his life the agony was ceased and two of his assaulters dragged Casper to a cell and tossed him to the floor. For a moment he lay still on the floor, breathing heavily trying to ignore the taste of blood in his mouth and the pain of broken parts all over the place.

"Oh sweet Jesus…" a voice said. Casper looked up using most of his effort and was bewildered to find Harper looking down at him.

"Ha…Harper?" Casper breathed. He nodded and still looked shocked but didn't move toward him. Casper decided he would go to him but quickly another voice stopped him. Out of the shadows beside Harper came Maverick, bruised and tired but concerned for him.

"Don't come any closer, Cass, you can't see it but there's some kind of energy wall between us and you," Maverick explained. Casper nodded slowly and settled for rolling onto his back so as not to cause more pain to his chest. "Are you alright?" Maverick asked.

"I'm still breathing…barely," Casper coughed. "Man…" he groaned. "They beat the shit out of me."

"Those goddamn animals..." Maverick cursed. It was then he winced and leaned heavily onto Harper who helped him sit down.

"Mav? What did they do to you?" Casper coughed. He struggled to get to his feet and get as close as possible to the force field.

"I'm alright, Cass, don't strain yourself worrying about me, sit back down," Maverick breathed. Casper slowed his approach slightly and got back onto his knees but still looked at his brother.

"The last time they dropped you off you weren't conscious and Maverick tried to get to you but they...subdued him," Harper explained.

"Cracked a few ribs too," Maverick breathed heavily.

"Last time? How many times have I been in and out of here?" Casper asked.

"Three or four times," Harper replied. "I wanted to stop them but..."

"It's okay, there was nothing you could have done." Casper sighed. He looked down at his torn uniform and saw he had clearly borne the brunt of any attack on the three of them. "I wanted to be popular amongst people I know but this is ridiculous." He sighed. Despite the pain he got to his feet and started slowly pacing back and forth.

"Casper, you should rest," Maverick said.

"I can't. I sit still and my mind will want to rest, my mind rests and I can't focus, I can't focus and I can't get out of here, we don't get out of here and we die, we die and well...I can't let that happen, so I can't sit still," Casper explained. Pacing was trying on his aching body but keeping the pain fresh was keeping him awake and focused.

"Sometimes you scare me," Harper said. Casper looked at him and shook his head.

"Sometimes I scare myself." He sighed.

"I still think you should take it easy. I'm sure Mom and Dad are sending a rescue party as we...what's so funny???" Maverick asked. The second he mentioned rescue party both Harper and Casper burst out laughing, even though for Casper, it was tremendously painful. In fact, it took him several slow deep breaths to be able to speak again.

"Mav, you just stick to politics okay?" Casper smiled. Seeing his brother's confused face he decided to elaborate a little. "This isn't the palace, Mav, this isn't the safe home we know. You wanted to know what *my* life is like, well you're living it, my friend. In this world we have to rely on one person and that's yourself."

"I should think we can trust each other," Maverick said. Harper shook his head.

"Negative, we all see each other and think we're all together but these fanatics have been known to play mind games with serums and drugs. For all I know you two are trying to get information from me," Harper replied. As a joke he narrowed his eyes at the two men and eyed them suspiciously. Casper laughed but Maverick did not.

"How can you two joke at a time like this? We've been captured by the enemy! We're in some real danger!" Maverick exclaimed. Casper stopped laughing and looked at his brother and felt bad. Maverick had never been in this kind of heart-stopping situation where you didn't know if you were going to die or not. He could see the fear and uncertainty in his brother's eyes and sighed. Casper got as close as he could to the wall without actually touching the force field.

"This situation just has to be dealt with one step at a time, Mav. There's no point in panicking because it's already happened. Now we should be focusing on how to stay alive," Casper said softly. He spoke slowly because he wanted his brother to understand he did see the seriousness of the situation and was concerned but not scared.

"Alive? What about getting out of here?" Maverick asked.

"Let's not get ahead of ourselves, Maverick, we need to be sure we have time to think of an escape before we plan one. Heck, they could come in any minute now and wipe the three of us out," Harper supplied helpfully. Casper made a face of exasperation at Harper and shook his head, then looked back to Maverick who had lowered his head in despair.

"It'll be okay, Mav, I promise. I'm not going to let your first military experience be your last," Casper said. He smiled at the joke trying to be gentle about it but when Harper started howling in laughter he had no choice but to join in.

They had quieted down several hours later. There was no way of knowing what time of day it was or where they were because of the dark cells they sat in. Casper had settled slightly and sat leaning against the wall of his cell. He looked up at the black ceiling trying to imagine how they could get out, but so far his mind was as blank as the ceiling above him.

Harper had kicked back on a blanket that had been put on the floor for sleeping on and had his hands crossed behind his head. It always amazed Casper how his friend could relax and fall asleep on anything. Maverick had been the one who took to pacing now and was going up and down and up and down the small cell.

"Maverick, you're my prince and everything, but that fucking pacing has *got* to stop," Harper said from under his arm.

"I can't help it, I've never been in a situation I can't negotiate out of," Maverick replied.

"No one said negotiation was out of the question." Harper sighed.

"I doubt these monsters even know what diplomacy is," Maverick snorted. At this Harper took his arm off his face and looked up at Maverick.

"These *monsters* are simply doing what they were told to do. They're fighting for what they believe in, as are we, it doesn't make us better than they are, and it doesn't make them better then us," Harper explained. Casper always thought soldiers came out with things that made more sense than any politician and this time was no different.

"Are you siding with the enemy??" Maverick accused. Harper rolled his eyes and then closed them again.

"Believe whatever you want, Prince." He sighed. Again most soldiers seemed to show a lot more patience than a politician. Casper decided not to get involved in their conversation, instead he decided to concentrate on the slight noises around him.

More precisely a slight hissing noise that was getting louder. Casper had no idea for how long it had been going, but he was sure it hadn't been in the room when he came to. What *was* that noise?

"Guys," Casper said finally. Both men stopped what they were doing and looked at him.

"What is it, Casper?" Harper asked. Casper stood wearily and started to look around him in concern.

"Do you hear that?" he asked. The hissing had started to increase and the air in his cell was becoming slightly stale.

"Hear what?" Maverick asked. Casper looked to the floor and saw the air wasn't just getting stale, it was changing color!!

"Holy shit," Harper exclaimed.

"What is it?" Maverick asked. Both men stood and got as close as they could to the wall looking into Casper's cell.

"Why is it only in your cell?" Harper asked. The slightly gray tinted smoke was rising ever so slightly.

"I...don't...know," Casper said. The air was thickening, he could feel it start to burn in his lungs, breathing became much harder. Casper started to cough trying to shield his face from the smoke.

"Casper, hang on, Cass!!" Maverick exclaimed. What the hell was going on?? What ever this smoke was, it was burning his lungs, he couldn't breathe! He was slowly being suffocated! The effort was too much to stand as Casper dropped on all fours and started to spit and cough the foul-tasting smoke from his lungs.

"Can't...breathe..." he choked.

"Oh Jesus...oh god...Casper hang on, HANG ON!!" Maverick yelled. It must have been killing him to watch this smoke slowly kill his brother. This time Casper didn't even have enough to reply, he slowly sank to the floor, gasping for air. Soon the gasping turned to wheezing as Casper clawed at his throat to try and get some air into his lungs.

Just when he thought he was going to kiss his world goodbye, the cell door opened and two men walked in. They seemed to just look at Casper writhing on the floor as if they were waiting for something to happen. Possibly waiting for him to die.

"HELP HIM DAMN IT!!" Maverick screamed. The men didn't even give Maverick or Harper a second glance, but continued to stare at Casper.

Finally breathing started to get a little easier, the smoke started to dissipate out of the cell.

"Hawk, you okay?" Harper asked. Casper nodded as he breathed deeply and sucked in some fresh air that was being pumped into the cell.

"Better," he breathed at him. Finally he had enough energy to stand to face the men outside the cell. He glared at them viciously.

"Have fun watching?" he growled. "Hope you got off as much as you wanted." The two men looked at each other and then opened the cell door. Casper wasn't sure if he had just incited a riot or what was going on, but in any case, the two men were bigger than him and had weapons. He backed into the corner of his cell making sure they couldn't get behind him and got ready to fight to the bitter end.

"Leave him alone!!" Harper exclaimed. "Take me on, you stupid fucks! I dare you!" His offer went unnoticed as the two men started in on Casper. They moved very slow, but Casper knew he had to wait for them to make the first move...which they did. One man grabbed Casper's arm and spun him around slamming him into the wall. Before Casper had time to react his other hand was grabbed and shoved behind him. He felt binders being placed on his skin and knew he was completely helpless as they slammed him to the ground on his stomach.

"Do it," one man said. Even though his face was being shoved down so all he could do was look at the others, he knew he was in trouble when both Harper and Maverick's faces went white.

"Stay away from him!" Maverick yelled. It was no use, Casper suddenly felt a hypo-spray pressed into his neck.

At first there was nothing, his body simply mellowed, almost like he was on some sort of relaxant. Maverick and Harper looked at him and he looked back, for some reason he didn't say anything he just stared. Then the burning sensation began, in his feet, his legs, his torso, his lungs, his neck, and finally his head.

Casper started screaming trying to get rid of the pain that burned through him. It hurt so much! He tried to struggle away from his captors but they held him fast.

"OH GOD!!" Casper bellowed. "Kill me please!! It hurts!!" He hadn't meant to sound so desperate but at this point, he would rather welcome death than continue to suffer.

"Hang on, Cass! Hang on! We'll get you out of there!" Whether it was Harper or Maverick who said it, Casper didn't know if he'd be alive to see their escape. Finally Casper couldn't take it anymore, his eyes rolled back, his tongue dropped down and he welcomed the bliss of darkness...

CHAPTER FOUR

Casper was back on the bridge of his ship, he was watching a fierce battle go on in front of him on the view screen.

"Report," Casper said calmly.

"We've had a sector breach over by the *Countess*' position," Harper replied. "Four ships have gone to intercept and they're reporting…they can't find them." Casper looked at him wide-eyed.

"They can't find the enemy? Tell them to open their eyes and look out the window!" he shouted. Harper shook his head sadly,

"They can't find the *Countess*, she's gone…they're reporting debris, sir…fuck the *Countess* has been destroyed," he replied. Casper closed his eyes and shook his head, almost like a moment of silence for the lives lost.

"Any survivors?" he asked.

"None, sir, they were blind-sided," Harper replied. At this Casper raised an eyebrow.

"Blind-sided? How is that possible? The *Countess* had the best sensors of the fleet," he said.

"Clearly not good enough." Harper sighed.

"Captain, the crew of the *Nautilus* is hailing us," Linda informed him. He gave her a quick nod to patch them through. Commander Lexis had a grave look on his face.

"How you holding up, Commander?" Casper asked.

"Not so well, we are proud men are we not?" Lexis asked. Casper was confused but decided to play along.

"That we are, my friend, what do you need?" Casper asked. Lexis sighed, closed his eyes and shook his head.

"We've taken heavy damage as you are aware, and I am never one to back down from a fight or retreat but…as hard as this is for me to request…" Lexis sighed.

"Your crew is running on its last legs, correct?" Casper asked. Again Lexis nodded somberly.

"We've many injured, more than we do healthy, my soldiers are working double and triple shifts to keep in this fight, Captain Hawk," he explained. Casper could see the man was hurting mentally, the *Nautilus* had suffered a lot in the past couple days; Casper was well aware of this.

"Commander, you have my full permission to pull out of formation and head for home a few weeks early. I've lost two ships, and I'd rather not lose any more. Go with my blessing friend, I'll see you back there," Casper said. He could see the look of relief on the commander's face but also one of sorrow that he was backing out early. "Commander?"

"Yes, sir?"

"The best leaders know when they have reached their limits, Commander, there is no shame in taking your soldiers home to their families," Casper said. At his comment, Lexis seemed to brighten up a little and nod his thanks and respect toward Casper.

"You're a good man, Captain Hawk, thank you," he said. With that the communication was cut and the *Nautilus* broke ranks in the direction of home.

When Casper finished watching the ship disappear from the ranks on his sensors, he looked up to find Linda looking at him with a big smile.

"What?" he asked.

"And people say you're a hard ass," she smiled. Casper shook his head and turned toward the view screen.

"Incoming torpedo!" Harper exclaimed.

"All hands brace for impact!" Casper alerted. He sat in his chair and held on tight as the ship was violently shaken back and forth. Sparks started to fly up in various areas of the bridge and Casper had to shield his eyes. That last hit had been a bad one, and if they didn't get out of here fast they'd be space dust. "Report!!" Casper exclaimed.

However, when he was met by silence he turned to his right side where he was about to rip a strip from Harper for not answering. *Was about to*... Harper wasn't in his seat but rather clawing his way back into it as a stream of blood ran down half his face. Casper could see Harper's right arm was badly burned, the uniform sleeve completely burned off. It was clear that Harper was shaken quite a bit and trying to figure out where the sensor *was* let alone what the report was.

"The...uh...ships..." Harper slurred. He was confused, Casper could see that.

"Harp, step away from the panel and let someone else take over," he said.

"I'm...good...really," Harper slurred. Casper shook his head and got up from his chair and walked over beside Harper and helped him out of the chair.

"Brant, you have the bridge," he said. Then he helped Harper to the infirmary. Halfway there Harper's legs started to give out on him.

"I'm...sorry...I can't..." Harper's words were few and far apart, he was struggling to just put one foot in front of the other.

"S'alright buddy, I got you come on." Casper smiled. He lifted Harper over his shoulder and carried him to the infirmary, all the way there reassuring and making sure Harper was still with him.

Once he reached the infirmary the doctor took care of him right away. Casper meanwhile sat down and took a breather, he had been up for thirty-two hours and it was starting to get to him. The doctor came up and smiled as only she could smile.

"Technically, I could have put you under a day ago and be completely clear in doing so," she said.

"I'm fine, Doc, just a little tired is all, haven't had much time to sleep," he replied.

"Sir, all due respect, you need sleep to lead, and I can't in good conscience let you leave this room without you sleeping for at *least* two hours. On your own or by force, you're going to sleep… uh…sir," the doctor said harshly. Casper shook his head and lay down on the bio-bed that he sat on.

"Drug me, Doc," he said. She smiled and brought a hypo-spray into his line of view and brought it up to his neck. "I hate those things," he said. "I mean it's great what they do but…I don't like that sting." The doctor smiled and put her hand on his shoulder soothingly.

"Well I have a magic touch, and I can take away the pain with a little trick," she said. Casper raised an eyebrow and looked at the cloth she pulled from a nearby table. She rubbed it on his neck and he felt a cool sensation but nothing more. He blinked and then noticed she was putting the hypo-spray down.

"Hey, what about the injection?" he asked. The doctor winked at him and smiled.

"We're done, sir," she replied. "I told you I had the magic touch that's a little mixture I made up to numb the area."

"You're a saint," Casper smiled wistfully. He yawned and closed his eyes and drifted off into a peaceful, welcome, gentle…

…cold. He was shivering like never before and no matter how hard he tried he couldn't make it stop.

"…ink he's coming to," someone said.

"…come on, Cass, you can do it…"

"…Fight it, Hawk, come on…FIGHT IT." Suddenly Casper was awake. It had been his friend and brother he heard encouraging him. Now it was all an issue of opening his eyes and letting them know he was alright. He couldn't, however, he was too damn cold and needed all his energy to keep him warm.

"C, cold, d," he slurred quietly.

"What? Did he say something?"

"I don't know, I thought I heard something."

"Do it again, Casper, let us know you're still with us." Casper shivered but he heard their pleas and tried again.

"C, cold..." he said a bit louder.

"I heard it that time, come on let's see if we can warm him up." Casper felt arms on him and then some kind of material being placed over his chest. There was some added warmth, but still Casper was feeling very cold. He tried to think of how to let the men know he was still freezing, but he still didn't have enough energy to say so.

Oddly enough, he felt something at that moment that he hadn't felt in many, many years; he wanted his mom. For some reason or another he had an overwhelming urge to be held by the woman who held him for every scraped knee and bump on the head. Now more than ever he wished he had stayed home, stayed with his mother on that bed and talked to her like she wanted. Now he may never again get that chance; a chance he figured he'd have years to do.

"Mom..." Casper cried quietly. A tear slid absentmindedly from his closed eye and he shivered alone on the ground. Then in his vulnerable state, he felt two strong arms wrap around him and lift him slightly so he lay in someone's lap.

"I've got you, Cass." Maverick's voice was soft but strong, he must have heard Casper's silent wish and was trying to fulfill it as best he could.

Casper could hear his older brother's heart beat and felt the warmth radiating off him. The closeness and the generally warm feeling physically and mentally that Casper was feeling caused the shivering to slowly stop. He was starting to warm up and finally managed to open his eyes.

His vision was quite blurry, but he could make out the arms around him and close by his side was Harper, looking worried but relieved that Casper was awake. Casper looked up at his brother who held him much like a mother and her child.

"Mav...?" Casper began.

"Just warm up first." Maverick smiled. Many things went through Casper's mind as he saw tears welling up in Maverick's eyes. The unexpected show of strong emotion also brought many questions into Casper's mind, particularly how long he had been unconscious or in whatever state he had been. There were so many questions he wanted to ask, but at the moment he didn't have the energy. He settled instead for clutching his brother's arm burying his face in the man's warmth and falling asleep.

What must have been several hours later Casper woke, feeling much better than he had earlier. He looked around him and found both Maverick and Harper were asleep. Gently sliding out of his brother's arms, Casper stood to stretch his legs. It turned out he was much weaker than he first imagined which made him question again how long he had been unconscious. He also wondered how he, Harper and Maverick all got into the same cell.

"Hey, you're awake." Casper turned around to see Harper pulling himself up to lean on the wall. He yawned, looked at Casper and smiled.

"Yeah, I feel weird but better than before," Casper replied. He went up to Harper and sat against the wall beside him. When his eyes met Harper's he saw something he never thought possible in his best friend and best soldier's eyes—fatigue. After all they had been through and after all the wars they had fought, never had Casper seen fatigue in Harper's eyes. Something else Casper noticed, Harper *and* Maverick looked rather unkempt, as if they had been sitting there for awhile.

"Y'alright?" Harper asked with a tired smile.

"Harper…tell me honestly, how long has it been?" Casper asked. Harper sighed, lowered his head and shook his head slightly.

"I, I don't really know." Harper sighed. "I'd like to tell you, but there's just no way to know how long."

"You have to have some idea," Casper asked. "Hours, days, weeks…*months?*" Harper shook his head, sharply this time.

"Casper, I don't know!" he replied. "They've been moving you in and out, in and out…we weren't paying attention to the time, okay? We were paying attention to making sure you were alive!" Casper could see his friend was exhausted and knew he had no right to demand anything. While he had been unconscious for, however long it had been and whatever had happened, they had not. Harper and Maverick had witnessed every moment.

"I'm sorry," Casper said quietly. Harper looked up and smiled weakly but still with much fatigue evident in his face.

"It's okay," Harper replied. "I'm just really, really tired, Casper. I can't say how long it has been but I can tell you it's been too long." Casper put his hand on Harper's head and ruffled his hair to try and lighten the man's attitude.

"Well, time to plan our way out now," he said. It was then Harper looked up at him, his eyes full of uncertainty.

"I…I don't think I can," he replied quietly. Casper was shocked.

"Man, what did they do to you?" he asked. He didn't wait for the answer however before grabbing his shoulders and squeezing them tightly. "You can, Harper, we can. The three of us will kick some ass and then run like hell until we get on a ship and get home." However, Harper swallowed hard and looked away from Casper to Maverick. His eyes showed confusion and worry, a frightened individual who just didn't know what to do.

"I don't think we've all got the energy for that," Harper whispered. His voice had been so low he barely heard it, but he did and was afraid to know more. Casper looked at his sleeping brother and wondered what had happened. Casper felt tears well up in his eyes as to the possible meanings of Harper's comment.

"Harper…what's wrong with my brother?" he asked. Harper buried his face in his hands as if trying to hide from the question; when he looked up his eyes were empty and stoic. It was the face of a soldier who had seen something so horrible he just couldn't figure out how to react.

"I tried to stop them," he whispered. Casper's heart started to beat faster and faster.

"Sean-Patrick, you need to tell me what happened," he repeated. Harper looked back over to Maverick who still hadn't woken up.

"The took him away for a long time," Harper started. "When they brought him back they dumped him on the floor…" Harper stopped struggling to remain stoic with the story. "He's wearing thin, Cass, I really don't think he can take much more of this. I mean, look at us." Casper shook his head and looked at the ground; they hadn't even been told as to why it was they were being held. He had some idea but as to the particulars he had no idea. Slowly, Casper moved over toward his brother despite the fatigue to his own body. He was just so damn tired.

When Harper joined him at Maverick's side, the sleeping man stirred slightly and opened his eyes. However, when he saw Casper, Maverick was wide awake and burst into tears clutching his brother's sleeve. As a soldier and never being very close to his family, Casper was caught off guard and took a few seconds before he could react and hug his brother back.

"I thought I'd never speak to you again," Maverick cried into his brother's sleeve.

"Easy, Mav, I'm right here, I'm not going anywhere," Casper soothed. He looked up at Harper who was looking away in shame and pity. Emotions to which Casper faulted him not, the man had every reason to try and not feel the very emotions that would simply kill him faster in a place like this.

Just then there was a hiss and their cell door opened. Casper waited for someone to come in but no one did. More curious still, the hall they stared down seemed to be empty of any personnel.

"This isn't right," Harper said in a low quiet voice.

"No, it's not, but let's use this to our advantage shall we?" Casper replied. Harper looked at him and seemed uncertain.

"It's got to be a trap," he said. Casper nodded, clearly he was going to have to be the toughest one in this situation because fortunately for him he knew nothing of the past several days.

"Maybe so but still, we're Royal Guard, Harp, you and I have taken on worse. We can do this, but I need the two of you to stick with me," Casper said sternly. After a moment of hesitation Harper relented and nodded his head.

"With you to hell and back, sir," he replied. Now the convincing was needed of the man Casper worried about the most. Maverick, although strong willed, was not a soldier, nor a killer, therefore, might be a little harder to convince.

"Mav, look at me," Casper said. Maverick looked up, eyes still filled with an over flow of tears. "You have to be with me on this, do you hear me? I'll get you out of here but you have to move when I say to okay?" Maverick's eyes were that of a little lost boy: scared, unsure, ashamed at his lack of confidence, and embarrassed that he was crying. Casper tried to fight back the uncomfortable feeling that threatened him in his stomach; he had never seen his brother like this before, never so cowardly.

By no means did he blame his brother for being scared, considering the life Maverick was used to it was amazing he had even dared sneak aboard a royal ship.

"Don't fight me on this, Mav, I need you with me do you understand? You can do this because Harper and I will be with you every step of the way," Casper added. On Maverick's other side Harper had also grabbed onto him and had erased the embarrassed look from his eyes.

"You and your brother are from a bloodline of royals, in your veins are war heroes, political geniuses, and a strong, valiant family name. Get on your feet and fight your way out for every man and woman that has ever lived with the Hawk name," Harper said with poise. Maverick swallowed hard and then looked to Casper, without a word and a heavy sigh, he nodded and started to his feet.

Before Maverick was fully up, Casper knew he was very weak and helped him appropriately. His brother had clearly suffered a great deal more then he during the whole or ordeal.

Those thoughts shoved aside, Casper had already started forming a list of "to do's" in his head. One, they needed weapons; two, they needed a way out; three, they needed a ship. All this in his head, they three men crept down the hallway being ever so cautious not to make a sound. Casper knew someone had opened the door on purpose, and he knew someone probably wanted him to get out, but it was the 'why' that was the big question.

"Jackpot!" Casper turned to face Harper who was looking at one of the panel sensors along the hallway. "Someone wants us out of here," he added. He pointed to the panel and upon joining him, Casper saw it was a map of the entire ship.

"Let's get out of here before someone changes their mind," he whispered. Harper nodded and taking Maverick's arm once again they set off now knowing full well where they had to go.

Their entire journey down to the launch bay was without incident which raised a great number of questions but at the same time gave Casper and his colleagues a bit more confidence.

Inside the shuttle bay they found two ships, one a ship they didn't recognize and the second... Casper froze. The second ship wasn't just any ship, it was a royal shuttle from his own ship!

"They stole my own goddamn shuttle!" Casper growled.

"Uh, maybe we should talk about this later?" Harper breathed. Casper looked back at him holding up Maverick and mentally kicked himself for thinking of his ship at a time such as this.

"Right," he said. "Let's go." They quickly boarded the shuttle and closed the door. Maverick moved to a corner of the shuttle and curled himself into the fetal position. Casper sighed but knew he had no time to worry about Maverick at the moment, he'd do that later, right now they were still onboard with the enemy.

"Shit, Cass, we've got company." Casper whirled around to the main view screen and saw several men in dark uniforms running toward the shuttle.

"It's about time," he mumbled. Harper shot him a look.

"You're excited??" he asked.

"No, I just knew it couldn't be this..." before Casper could finish, something rocked the shuttle. Casper jumped into the other pilot's chair and started flipping on switches. "Oh no...you're not getting me after letting us go this far," Casper said. "Arm weapons, Harper, they don't want us out, we'll shoot out."

"Already done," Harper said. Casper could hear his friend's voice shaking ever so slightly with adrenaline and fear.

"Fire at anything that moves," he said. He had barely finished speaking when Harper's itchy trigger finger let loose a torrent of laser shots in every possible direction. Finally anyone outside the ship was dead or in hiding, but Harper was still firing wildly. "Harp...Harper...Sean! Cease fire!" After standing up and grabbing Harper's hand the man finally stopped and took a deep breath.

"Sorry," he said quietly.

"It's alright, let's just get out of here," Casper replied. He jumped back into the pilot's chair and finished prepping the launch commands. Once the ship was ready, they blasted out the bay doors and in minutes were in the wide open liberty of the cosmos.

"Where are we going?" Harper asked. Casper turned to look at him almost confused by the question as if the answer should be blatantly obvious.

"Home, why? Did you have other plans?" Casper smiled weakly. After a brief pause Harper smiled and shook his lowered head. "Do me a favor, Harp?" Casper asked.

"You saved my life again, Casper, anything," Harper replied.

"Keep a close eye on Mav, until we get back." Harper stood and nodded.

"Now that I can do." He smiled and traipsed back into the ship and out of sight. Casper checked the sensors again and again, making sure they weren't being followed or scanned. Nothing, absolutely nothing; this wasn't right at all, and Casper was starting to get very nervous as to why they had been set free.

After a while, however, his inhibitions died down a little and he put the shuttle on autopilot so he could go check on the other two. In the bay of the shuttle, Harper had managed to get Maverick onto one of the beds but the man still sat in the fetal position hugging his knees. When Casper approached them, only Harper looked up with a sad look and stood.

"I can barely get a word," he whispered.

"Let me try," Casper replied. He sat at the end of the bed facing Maverick and making sure he was at least at eye level. "Hey Mav," Casper started, his brother didn't move. "I know this is scary but we're on our way home now…" Casper wasn't quite sure what to say to his brother because he never in a million years thought he'd be the one to comfort the man after a situation such as this.

"He's really shaken up, they scared the bejesus out of him." Harper sighed.

Casper frowned, the idea that his brother had been subjected to probably a lot more than he ever thought possible, made him sick. They knew Maverick was the politician and not the soldier; they knew he had never fought a battle in his life that wasn't on paper.

"Mav, I promise you they won't get away with this, retribution will be ours, you hear me?" Casper asked. Finally Maverick responded slightly and raised his head to look at Casper.

"I don't want retribution…" he said almost in a murmur.

"What do you want?" Casper asked.

"For it never to have happened," Maverick replied. All over again his eyes began to fill with tears, and he looked away from the two men in shame. "How can you be so strong after what's happened?" he cried.

"We're soldiers," Harper jumped in. "We've seen this kind of action since we joined up. It's okay for you to feel scared."

"I'm not scared!" Maverick hissed. This caught both Casper and Harper off guard. They sat back a little and waited for an explanation. Maverick took a deep breath, "Well…maybe I am a little, but I'm more angry."

"That's expected, I'm downright pissed off that that bastard lied when he said he'd take only me," Casper replied. Bernard Atkinson was never a man to be trusted; Casper had learned that quite quickly. There was no telling what had happened to the other men and women.

"I'm pissed off I didn't get to take a chunk out of that man's hide," Harper added.

"All in due course, my friend." Casper nodded to him.

"I'm angry because there was nothing I could do to stop them," Maverick said quietly. Casper and Harper both looked at him curiously.

"Stop them? Maverick, what did they do to you?" Casper asked. At this, Maverick looked the two men in the eye as his own eyes grew huge with grief.

"I…" Maverick began. "I…I can't…" It was almost as if whatever he had seen was so terrible that his mind was shutting out the memory. Casper took his brother's shoulder and gave it a squeeze.

"Hey, it's okay, when you're ready," he said quietly. He stood up and sat on the other bed across from Maverick. He was suddenly feeling very tired. The adrenaline of the escape had left him and he barely had energy to stand up.

"Why don't you rest up, I still have to figure out how far we've got to go," Harper offered. Casper nodded his thanks and was already half asleep on the bed.

Casper was back on the beach by the castle lying down looking up at the gorgeous blue sky. Beside him Isis lay barely clad in a swim bikini hugging his arm with her eyes closed peacefully. Casper turned slightly so he could look at her better, which made Isis smile sweetly and open her eyes.

"What?" she asked with a laugh.

"I can't help it, you're much prettier than anything out here, so I figured I'd stare at you," Casper replied. Isis smiled and then burst out laughing. She slapped him on the shoulder playfully.

"Well aren't you the charmer!" she said.

"I try," Casper feigned importance. "You know they teach us that stuff in prince school." Again, Isis burst out laughing then wrapped her arms around Casper's mid section.

"Don't ever change, love, don't ever change and we'll be together forever." She sighed. Casper smiled, he was about to close his eyes to take a nice rest when suddenly, out of nowhere the tide started to pick up. Along with that the skies darkened and the wind became violently strong. "What the hell is going on?" Isis screamed.

"I don't know! Come on, let's find cover!" Casper yelled. They began racing up the beach back to their car. In the parking lot, Casper could see Harper with the car doors open waving them over quickly. Isis got there slightly ahead of Casper and jumped in the car, but before he could follow Harper slammed the door.

"Harp, what are you doing? We have to get out of here," Casper exclaimed. However, Harper turned around revealing it wasn't Harper at all but Bernard Atkinson! "What are you doing here??" Casper demanded angrily.

"Sorry, Prince, it's the end of the road for you!" Bernard said. Then he jumped in the car and started to drive away. Casper panicked; Isis was still in the car! A horrible howling from behind him caught his attention, Casper turned just in time to get a glance of the tornado that was about to rip him from the planet.

Casper tried to find cover or at least something to hold on to but it was no use, he was taken into the air like a rag doll. As he was pulled every this way and that his only thought was of his family and beloved Isis whom he'd never see again.

"Cass, wake up, wake up!"

"*Isis!! Noooooooooooo!!!*" Casper shot straight up in the shuttle bed, his heart pounding, his lungs struggling for air and a thin layer of sweat drenching him from head to toe. Beside him Maverick was sitting up looking at him with great concern.

"Are you alright?" he asked. After several relaxing breaths Casper finally managed a nod.

"Bad dream…very bad dream," he sighed.

"Want to talk about it?" Maverick asked.

"Want to talk about what happened back in that prison?" Casper replied. He hadn't meant to be harsh or anything he just had no wish to explain his horrible dream. His plan worked much too well as Maverick went dead silent and looked back to the wall. "Look, Mav, I'm sorry. I…" Violently the ship shuddered from side to side. Maverick's face went ghost white and he nearly hit the roof. After making sure his brother wasn't going to pass out, Casper raced forward to the command central only to find Harper calmly sitting back drinking a hot cup of coffee.

"*Harper*!?!?!?" Casper exclaimed. Harper nearly dropped his steaming liquid all over himself in surprise but recovered and smiled.

"Easy, boss, nearly gave me a heart attack," he replied. "Did you know I graduated top of my class in navigation and weaponry?" Casper was about to ask what in the hell he was talking about, but then Harper pointed to the view screen. What Casper saw made his heart going into a jazz rhythm.

In front of them was nearly half the royal fleet, and the lead ship, the Spartan, had attached a cable to their shuttle reeling them in.

"Unfortunately com is down, so I can't get a word out to them, but I really didn't think it mattered," Harper said.

"No, it really doesn't," Casper smiled. "Come on let's go break the news to Maverick."

A few minutes later their shuttle was docked inside the Spartan, they had barely been in not ten seconds when a flurry of armed soldiers flooded the room, weapons raised and ready. It was standard protocol for any object that wasn't expected when brought aboard a military vessel, so Casper thought nothing of it.

After all the soldiers were settled in good firing positions one more soldier entered the room. Casper smiled as Commander Danielle Tyson strode into the room, her rifle slung over her shoulder and a look of determination on her face.

"Let's go say hello shall we?" Casper asked.

"Don't even have to ask me twice." Maverick smiled. It was good to see a bit of a healthy pigment return to his brother's face.

"Damn right, try and stop me," Harper added. Casper pushed open the shuttle door and stepped out, tired, disheveled, and weary. It mattered little as the three men were home.

The looks on all the soldiers' faces were priceless. Some looked at one another to make sure they weren't hallucinating, others stared on in wide-eyed shock and some had lowered their weapons in surprise. Danielle's eyes were huge, and she stood frozen for a second, then she slung her rifle and approached the three men.

"Captain Hawk?" she asked incredulously. Casper smiled and gave a nod.

"You have room on this ship for three lowly passengers?" he asked. Danielle bellowed out a loud "ah ha!" and then literally lifted Casper off his feet in a huge bear hug. Even though he was being slightly crushed, Casper didn't care, he was glad to be among friends again.

Still with an arm over Casper's shoulder Danielle turned to her soldiers. "Set a course for home, tell them we've got all three of them back alive!" she said. The room erupted in cheers as the crowd started to disperse back to their duties. However, her comment had made Casper wonder something he had long since pushed to the back of his mind, how long *had* it been?

"We need to talk, Danielle," Casper said. She looked at him still a huge smile on her face and nodded.

"Of course, of course! But Doc's orders you need to get a rundown first..." she began.

"Lt. Harper and Maverick okay, but you and I need to talk now," Casper said. Danielle didn't question, not even for a second. She motioned for some medics to come and help Maverick and Harper.

"Hey, Hawk, are you coming with us?" Harper asked.

"I'll catch up, you two go ahead," Casper replied. Harper nodded and walked off after Maverick and the medical staff.

Finally Casper and Danielle were alone and decided to head to her ready room to talk privately. Once inside Danielle offered Casper a cup of tea and they sat down to talk.

"We thought we'd never see you again." Danielle smiled.

"How long?" Casper said immediately. Danielle raised an eyebrow.

"Pardon?"

"Things happened to us, Dani, we were in and out of consciousness in a dark room...how long have we been missing?" Casper replied. The smile was gone from Danielle's face as she tried to imagine what could have possibly gone on during their abduction.

"Two months," she said quietly. Casper sucked in a deep breath and then let it out slowly and ran his hands through his hair. He knew it had to be more than a week or two but two *months*? That was longer than he thought possible.

"Wow." He sighed.

"Yeah," Danielle replied. "I can't begin to describe what it's done to the morale of the soldiers not to mention Hearth Condes." Casper looked up directly into her eyes.

"And my parents?" he asked. Danielle lowered her head and shook it slowly, her tightly tied hair bouncing side to side.

"Your father's taking it better than your mother. He's the one who organized eight ships to search for you," she replied.

"How'd you know where to look?" Casper asked.

"We asked your dad that same question, he said, 'everywhere until you're found,'" she explained. Casper smiled, it sounded like his father alright.

"And my mother, you said she isn't taking it so well?" he asked. Again Danielle shook her head.

"She's hiding it well from the public eye with help from Anthony, but she rarely speaks to anyone anymore. Last I heard she fainted, turned out she hasn't been eating much and keeps breaking into fits of tears for no reason. The poor woman was devastated when news came back from the transport and your own ship that the three of you had been taken," Danielle explained. Again Casper sucked in a deep breath and let it out slowly—his poor, poor mother. Oh how he wished he could be with her right at that moment.

"Two months," was all he could manage. Danielle shook her head and sighed, but then she lifted her head with a smile.

"But here you are now and things can get back to normal, the entire planet will be ecstatic to see the three of you again," she said. "Time to get you home." At the mention of home Casper couldn't help but smile, though he remembered very little, the ordeal was over and he was going to be reunited with his mom and dad.

"You have no idea how good that sounds." He smiled. "I should get back to Harper and Maverick."

"You could or you could wait here for a second," Danielle smiled. Casper raised an eyebrow wondering what it was she was planning. However, when the door behind them swooshed open his face lit up into a huge sunshine smile.

The woman in the doorway had covered her mouth in disbelief and happiness all at once. Then she rushed to him just as he stood and wrapped her arms around him.

"I thought I'd never see you again," Isis cried. Her sweet smelling hair was enough to bring tears of happiness to Casper's eyes as he held her tightly to him. As Danielle slipped out of the room he gave her a nod of thanks and then went back to his lady love.

"Don't cry, I'm alright now, it'll be okay," he said. Isis looked up at him, her striking eyes catching his in the dim light of the room.

"I love you, having you gone for those weeks…damn it, Casper, I love you." She smiled despite her tears. Casper smiled,

"Right back at you, babe." Then he slid his hand behind her soft neck and pulled her face toward him in a soft, welcome, gentle kiss. When they broke apart Casper took her hand.

"We should talk. Dinner?" he asked. Isis smiled and kissed his cheek with a nod and then they headed off to the mess hall.

CHAPTER FIVE

Danielle hadn't been kidding about the effect their abduction had on the planet. Word of their rescue got back before they did, so by the time they got there the streets from the landing pad to the palace gates were flooded with well-wishers and excitement. Casper looked out the window of his armored car and was amazed at the amount of people.

"You'd think we'd risen from the dead or something," he mumbled to himself.

"In a way we did." Casper turned to Harper who sat across from him.

"How so?" he asked.

"Well, we've been gone two months correct?"

"Yeah…"

"We were captured by the enemy, no?"

"Right…"

"An enemy who'd sooner see our heads on a stake than let us escape, yes?"

"With you so far…"

"So from all these people's point of view they had written us off, we were dead to these people and they were ready to move on without us, to survive as these strong people can. Then we show up not only alive but almost completely healthy? Tell me you wouldn't throw a party." Casper pondered what Harper was saying to him and then shrugged, it made sense. At the same time, there was only one person now that he wanted to provide solace to.

"My babies!!!" They had barely stepped out of the car when Patricia came running down the palace steps. The dress that she wore was bundled up in her hand, so she could run faster with out fear of tripping. Casper turned and opened his arms to her, moments later she dove into them and being the smaller of the two was lifted off her feet. He spun her once then put her down and hugged her.

"Oh, Ma, I'm so sorry," he said. Patricia pulled away and shushed him with a teary smile.

"It doesn't matter, you three are home now," she said. Then she turned to Maverick and pulled him into a huge hug weeping into his shirt. He smiled weakly trying to put on a brave face for her and hugged back.

"I love you, Mom," he said.

Next came Anthony. From the palace steps he hugged both his sons and then came back to Casper and put both hands on his shoulders. The old man's face was wrinkled into a smile and a glistening of tears glazed his eyes.

"You brave boys. I'm so proud you managed to make it back to your mother and me," he smiled.

"I learned from the best, Dad," Casper smiled. Anthony nodded and went over to Maverick to no doubt say similar things to him.

Casper turned to look at the crowd of people just outside the gates and smiled. There were at least three hundred people out there so as a token of his appreciation Casper waved to the crowd. The cheering that had been a mild din roared into a huge deafening cry of elation.

"Come, let's get the three of you inside. Harper, your father is waiting for you." Anthony smiled. Harper's mother had long since passed away when he was young, leaving Harper and his father to form a very tight relationship. At the mention of his father Harper's face lit up and he dashed up the palace steps taking them two at a time.

The rest of them followed, Casper slightly behind as he thought of what they had been through and still curious as to how they got out. Casper ran his hand through his hair, he was getting slightly tired and felt slightly warm. He attributed it to all the excitement, but then he started feeling dizzy; this wasn't a normal feeling at all.

"Something's wrong," he said. For safety's sake he decided to let the others know he wasn't feeling too good. His family and the nearby guards stopped and turned to him as he said this.

"Casper, what is it?" Anthony asked. Casper's breathing became slightly shallow, he really wasn't feeling too good at the moment but it didn't make sense. He had been fine a minute ago, and now he felt like he was going to pass out.

"I just…feel really…tired…" before he could say anymore the dizziness got to him and he wavered slightly only to be caught by his father.

"Come on the doctor will check you out," Anthony said with concern. All Casper could do was nod before feeling himself being lifted into his father's arms and carried the rest of the way.

After several tests Casper was finally resting comfortably in his own large bed, in his own room. It felt good to be home with all his own things around him. He figured his episode was due to stress because now he felt he was on the mend. Now he sucked on a nice glass of iced tea and was looking at one of his communication pads for information on the past two months.

"Can I come in?" Casper looked up to find Maverick standing in the doorway.

"Certainly," he said. He sat up a bit more in his bed so as to give Maverick more room to sit down. His brother sat and took up the panel that Casper had just put down.

"I didn't think we'd be missed so much," he said quietly.

"Yeah, we're celebrities, all the news for the past two months has had something to do with us," Casper replied. He could tell, however, his brother was just making idle chit chat and that the real reason he was there had yet to surface. "Hey Mav?"

"Yeah."

"It may sound weird but…I'm glad I wasn't alone on that ship, I don't think I could have made it through without you and Harper," Casper said. Maverick looked at him and let out a short sad laugh.

"Cass, if anything I should be saying that to you, really, when we were back in that prison I…" Maverick trailed off. He bit his bottom lip and tried to fight back tears, clearly he couldn't say anymore.

"God, I'm sorry Mav, whatever you were forced to endure I wish I could have been there for you," Casper sighed. Maverick shook his head, once, twice and again then looked at Casper.

"Don't you get it, you were there, through every horrible minute, you were right across from me after everything they did!" Maverick exclaimed. "You wanted to know what they did that was so awful? They made me believe you were dead." Casper sat up straighter and looked his brother right in the eye.

"Wh, what?" he asked. A tear slid down Maverick's face, and he wiped it away only to have another follow.

"The things they did to you…they made me watch…every scream, every empty look of death, every injection…they made me watch…" Maverick said quietly. Scream? Casper was positive he had been unconscious for the whole ordeal because all he remembered was his dreams. Dreams that had nothing to do with torture of any kind.

"But Mav, I don't remember being awake, you sure it was me?" Casper asked. "Harper said you were gone for awhile before I was conscious."

"I know…he told me that too…god I hope it wasn't you," Maverick sighed. "The screams…I just can't get them out of my head." Casper opened his mouth to say something, but his door opened and in came the doctor and their parents. None of them looked happy, they all in fact, looked quite devastated, clearly not good news.

"What is it?" Maverick asked. He saw the same look in their eyes that Casper did.

"Casper, dear…we uh…have some…news," Patricia said. She was trying to keep her emotions in check but wasn't doing a very good job.

"What?" Casper asked. He looked to the doctor who looked rather distraught.

"Well we ran some tests and the results…they aren't good," she said. "But make no mistake we're still checking blood samples and scans."

"Stop it," Casper said. "What is the problem?" The doctor drew in a deep breath and nodded.

"I don't know how else to say this but…there's a pathogen in your system." She sighed. Casper was confused and then it dawned on him.

"Wait…you're saying, they *infected me*?" he asked. The doctor looked to Casper's family and then back to him.

"Yes, I'm sorry to say, but it's a pathogen that's several strains of viruses combined and altered into one. It's literally attached itself to every cell in your body almost giving you a separate DNA altogether," she explained. Casper didn't know what to say, he didn't know what to think, he simply stood there in shock.

"What's going to happen to him?" Maverick asked. The doctor put her medical pad resting on her hip and sighed.

"It will gradually slow down the nervous system. The dizziness and fatigue and warmth you felt before were only mild symptoms of what's to come. You'll lose motor function of your limbs, your thought process will slow down and eventually stop. It's not a pretty thing, I won't sugar coat it any," she explained.

"So what do we need for the cure?" Casper asked. When he said this Casper's mother started crying into his father's shirt. The doctor was silent and looking at her feet and Anthony didn't seem to be looking at anything. "There isn't a cure," Casper deduced. Slowly and sadly the doctor nodded her head.

"No, but I've got everyone I can possibly think of looking for something," she said.

"No…no it can't be true," Maverick panicked. He stood up, his eyes wild with confusion.

"Maverick, easy now," Casper said. He had no idea but somehow keeping control of his brother was calming the own fire inside him.

"It wasn't you! It couldn't have been you! You said it yourself, Casper, it wasn't you!!" Maverick exclaimed. His step was getting quicker, his face getting ever so much more flush.

"Maverick, honey, don't over exert yourself," Patricia said.

"Over exert myself??? They made me watch mother!!! *They made me watch my own brother get tortured and injected and beaten time and time again. His face, you didn't see his face*!!" Maverick screamed. Casper got out of his bed and put a hand on his brother's shoulder.

"Mav, I'm still here, you need to calm down," he said. But Maverick seemed to have a wild look in his eye, he wasn't listening; he was reliving the past horrible moments he had endured much like Casper had done from the war. Casper looked to the doctor silently urging her to do something to calm him down. She seemed to get the message as she reached into her lab coat pocket and pulled out a hypo-spray.

"Maverick, I need you to sit down for me," the doctor said.

"Just do it, Doc, I got him," Casper said. The doctor nodded and brought the hypo-spray to Maverick's neck and pressed it in.

"Don't make me sleep…please…the… night…mares…" The injection hit Maverick and he started to slow down leaning heavily on Casper.

"It's okay, buddy, I gotcha, just relax," Casper soothed. Maverick's eyes closed and Casper was able to move his limp body onto the bed where he could sleep. Once his brother was down Casper turned to the doctor.

"How long do I have, Doc."

"*Casper*!" Patricia wailed. He knew she wouldn't like the question, but it was the only thing he could really see as relevant at the time.

"At best…eight weeks, nine if you take it easy," she replied. Casper closed his eyes and clenched his jaw, damn, that's why they had let him go…so his death could be more public.

"Plenty of time to find Atkinson and put his head on a stake," Casper said. He went over to his closet to find his military uniform. When he came back out his mother latched onto him.

"No, honey, no!" she whined. "You should be resting." Casper held her at arms' length and smiled.

"Mom…rest for what? Death? No thanks, I think I'll go out doing what I can," he said.

"Casper, over exerting yourself could lessen the amount of time you have. Even cut it in half…" the doctor started.

"Doc, I can't just lie in bed waiting for the end, I have to do something," Casper explained. He started to pull on his uniform shirt and do up the collar.

"Son…I don't agree with you leaving, but…I'll make sure your ship's ready to go," Anthony said. Casper was surprised but smiled at his father.

"Really? Thanks Dad, I…don't know what to say," Casper replied. Anthony nodded and came up to Casper and pulled his son into a hug. It was a surprising move because Anthony had never been a very physical father, more a pat-on-the-back, hand-shake kind of guy. This was different, Anthony was hugging him full fledged and filled with love.

"You take care of yourself, and you contact home as often as possible understand?" he said.

"Yeah, pop, I get it," Casper replied. They separated and Anthony took Patricia and they headed off with the doctor. Casper looked back at his brother sleeping on the bed as he finished getting dressed and felt bad, he might never see the man again. Casper literally had one thing keeping him going, Atkinson and the rage that boiled inside Casper's heart.

Casper narrowed his eyes and turned toward the door with as much gusto as he could muster.

"Time to go out with a bang, Cass," he said to himself.

Casper stood tall as he walked through the station toward the docking pad. It was clear by the murmurs and stares that the news had spread of his impending death sentence. Most looked at him with pity, others with sorrow and a sense of loss. Casper was tempted to yell that he wasn't dead just yet, but restrained himself as he headed to the brief room where he had been called moments earlier. He'd miss his home and the people, but at the same time he had no wish to stare at the ceiling waiting for death to come and get him.

He was doing the right thing, he knew it. As he walked down the hallways, he stood a bit taller in the pride that filled him. He was dying for a cause; his death wouldn't be meaningless.

"Kickin' ass and taking numbers," he smiled to himself. Casper was in the midst of pumping himself up and trying to forget the fact that he had little under three months to live when he stepped into the brief room. When he turned around he nearly jumped out of his skin when just over twenty-two men and women broke out into applause.

"What the deuce?" Casper exclaimed. Out of the crowd came Harper, Commander Danielle Tyson of the *Spartan*, and Captain Lexis of the *Nautilus*. When they came up to him Casper raised and opened his arms. "What's going on here?" he asked.

"When I found out your situation I spoke with some of the ships' captains…one thing led to another and voila, everyone here wants to come with you after Atkinson," Harper explained. Casper looked at the three in disbelief, and then looked at the men and women in the room incredulously.

"You…you're all here for me??" he asked. Everyone's head nodded with bright faces of support. Casper looked back to Lexis who stood in front of him.

"Captain Hawk, because of you, forty-six men and women who would have died aboard my ship, got the medical attention they needed and are now resting comfortably with their families. Countless others who were injured badly could return to their families and see home again. Sir, I honestly believe if it weren't for your kindness my ship would have joined the *Countess* and the *Magellan*. Myself and my crew will gladly follow you into the belly of the beast," Lexis said. Casper was blown away but deeply, deeply touched at the loyalty of his soldiers.

"Is this how you all feel?" he asked.

"To hell and back!" came the cry from the crowd. Finally the shock wore off and Casper smiled broadly and raised his hands to the crowd.

"Well then, let's stop wasting time and get out there!" he exclaimed. The crowd let out a cheer as they started to file out of the room toward the landing pads where their ships lay. They'd prepare them that day with supplies and armory then take off at first light. Casper made sure to shake hands and thank each and every one of his ships' captains as they walked by. His odds of finding Atkinson were now vastly improved because of the amount of people now standing behind him.

When the room was empty save Harper and Danielle, Casper was finally able to let his slight fatigue out.

"You sure you want to do this?" Harper asked.

"I can't back down now, not after all these people have devoted themselves to the cause; my cause." Casper sighed. "This has to be done." Harper smiled sadly and nodded, patting his friend on the shoulder.

"I wish this wasn't happening…and after I sat by while they did this to you…" He sighed. Casper returned the shoulder pat and shook his head.

"You did nothing wrong, Harp, you stuck by me like any captain can expect of a close friend," he said. Harper looked slightly relieved by what Casper had said and took a deep breath.

"Alright…well…let's get going!" he exclaimed. Casper nodded and watched Harper leave the room. He was about to follow when Danielle stopped him. The look on her face dredged up much curiosity in Casper.

"What is it, Danielle?" he asked.

"Do you really only have twelve months?" she asked quietly.

"Well, the way I'm pushing it now I think we can cut that time in half. I'm going for a record!" Casper joked. He chuckled to himself but stopped when he saw Danielle wasn't finding it as amusing as he. In fact she looked quite upset with Casper's situation. "It was a joke,

Dani, come on," Casper said. Danielle looked at him and for the billionth time that night Casper was caught off guard when a tear slid down her face.

"Casper, now that things are…well…that is to say…time is…" Danielle stumbled.

"Short?" Casper offered. Danielle silently nodded her head.

"I think there's something I need to tell you because I just can't let you die knowing I never said anything," she said. Danielle's eyes were slightly glazed with tears, Casper had rarely seen her like this, but she was a dear friend and he knew he couldn't bear to see her suffer.

"Hey, you can tell me anything, Dani, what's got you all choked up?" he asked. Slowly Danielle looked up at him and opened her mouth to speak but paused.

"This…" she said. Without a hint of a warning or even a heads up, Danielle leaned into Casper pressing him into the wall and with as much passion and yearning as she could muster. The kiss must have lasted for several seconds but all that Casper managed to focus on was the disbelief at what was happening.

Finally Danielle backed off, her face now flush with embarrassment.

"Wow," Casper breathed. He was trying to find the words and trying to find out how he felt deep down. "I mean really…wow."

"When Ensign Soul came to me and told me she was very concerned and wanted to see you I… Damn it, Casper, I got jealous that a younger, prettier, feistier girl managed to get to you before I did," Danielle sighed. Casper was sure his mouth almost hit the floor in amazement.

"How long have you felt like this?" he asked.

"Why do you think I've always been one step behind you in everything you do?" Danielle questioned back. Casper couldn't believe it, two women had confessed feelings for him almost all at once.

"Wow," Casper said.

"Yes, you said that already." Danielle smiled. She took his hand

and held it tightly in hers. "The ships are only being prepared today, we don't take off until morning."

"So?" Casper asked. Danielle leaned into him so he could feel her breath on his neck.

"Spend the night with me," she whispered. He was getting a proposition from his second in squadron command!!! Casper tried to think of what he should do. Isis would probably be waiting for him at her home for the night, but there was something about Danielle that drew him to her.

From since he could remember there were two reasons Danielle was referred to as a Greek goddess: one, her body, it was like she was built with the body of Aphrodite but the strength of Zeus. Two, no one touched her, ever, she'd drink with the men, eat with the men, flirt with the men, but no one ever managed to get anything more then a wink. Now here Casper stood with an offer to lay with her that night.

"Dani…wow…" was all Casper could manage.

"Casper, I can't watch you die knowing I never knew the pleasure of being with you mind, body, and soul…please…let me have this if nothing else, let me have this night," she asked.

"Isis…"

"Doesn't have to ever find out. If she's the one you want, then so be it. I'm not going to waste away pining for you, but I at least want a chance," Danielle interrupted. Casper looked down at her hands around his and took a deep breath, the woman's manipulation of her power was intoxicating.

"This is wrong, I know it is and yet…" Casper stopped. He looked up to Danielle's beautifully soft gray eyes and her tightly arranged hairline. This time he couldn't stop himself, *he* leaned in so as to receive yet another passionate kiss from her before breaking apart.

"You know where my room is, if you decide to come, it will mean more to me than you know," Danielle said. With a swift turn of her heals and bounce of her hair she was out the door and out of sight. Casper plopped himself back into one of the chairs in the room and tried to think clearly.

"What did Tyson want?" Harper stuck his head in the doorway a few seconds later and was looking at Casper. His timing couldn't have been better.

"Come in and close the door, I need someone to talk to and some how…you seem like the best man for the job," Casper said. Harper looked confused but sat down across from him and waited for Casper to begin.

A half hour later Harper was doubled over laughing in his chair and slapping his knee.

"You are a *trouble maker*!!" He howled. "You sly, sly dog you!!" he added. "Man! The Greek? You actually got an offer from The Greek!?!?! Wow…I should take lessons from you! Ladies dropping left, right and center for you!"

"Um…a little more decorum and respect for your fellow officers, Harp." Casper sighed.

"You're right, you're right," Harper said, calming himself down. "Okay…sorry it just caught me by surprise."

"That's alright," Casper said. "All I really want to know is what you think I should do."

"Well," Harper began. "Danielle's room is in the palace, a lot closer to get to than going into town to find…"

"Harper, you half wit! Just because she's closer doesn't mean I should go with her!" Casper groaned. After a snort of laughter Harper sighed and finally managed to calm down.

"Okay well what do you *feel* you should do?" he asked. Casper sighed and looked up at his friend, as if trying to find an answer in his face. Isis had made him feel special, and he'd like to give them a chance but at the same time Danielle had been his friend almost as long as Harper had, and she had almost begged him to be with her that night.

"I'm not sure, that's why I wanted a second opinion. We've known each other forever, Harp. You know me, I need some advice on this one," Casper replied. Harper leaned back in his chair and crossed his arms over his chest. After a pause he spoke again.

"You know if you were any other man I would say don't be an ass and either stick with Isis or break it off with her, but you aren't any other man."

"So are you saying I should go be with Dani and not tell Isis?" Casper asked.

"I'm saying we've been discussing this for the past forty-five minutes, I can't make the choice for you, Cass, because clearly you aren't even sure yourself. I guess there's only one way to remedy that," Harper shrugged. Casper thought about it for a moment and then took a deep breath.

"I see what you're saying," he replied. "I have to decide on my own." Harper nodded and then stood.

"Well, I have torpedoes to load and weapons to check, I'll see you at dawn." He smiled. Casper nodded and waved goodbye to his friend. He sat there for a long time thinking about what Harper had said and thinking about the situation in general. Then after much deliberation Casper came to a decision and stood up tall.

Later that night Casper sat in one of the guest rooms of the palace, his own room still was refuge to his older brother at the moment. When Maverick woke up, he didn't say a word, he didn't move, he just lay there like a traumatized victim would. Casper had decided to use the guest room rather than take over his brother's room out of respect or in case Maverick found his way to his own room late at night.

Now Casper sat in the chair thinking, he was weeks away from dying. He was about to depart on a mission come the morning and most likely never see his mother, father, or home again. There was no way of knowing if they'd even be able to find Atkinson and his gigantic cloaked ship. In which case, it could mean spending his last days searching and dying alone in space.

It was a morbid sad thought made that Casper take a deep breath and shake his head; he never thought at his young age of twenty-seven he'd be thinking of his death in a matter of weeks. A single tear slipped down his face, he was so alone in his ordeal. No one knew what he was going through mentally, emotionally, and most of all physically. He had already begun to notice the increased fatigue and the fact that it would be harder to push himself to keep going with every passing second. Whether or not that was a physical battle or emotional had yet to be determined.

Ding, ding. Casper looked toward his door and sighed.

"Come in," he said. The doors swooshed open and with more strut than Casper had ever seen Danielle came silently into his room. Although he had been her good friend for a long time he had never quite looked at her like he was now. In turn, Danielle had never dressed for him like she was now. Casper had no idea Danielle's hair was so long, but now the strawberry blonde had her hair out of its ties and it now went all the way down just below her waist. She wore a thin silk night gown that hugged her tall voluptuous figure very nicely.

"I got your message," Danielle said finally. "Are you sure?" she asked.

"I'm not sure about anything anymore," Casper said as he stood up. "I hope you don't think any less of me because of what I've said." Danielle came up to him and reached for the top button on his uniform.

"I'd never think any less of you, Casper, that's why I'm here," she whispered. Then she leaned in and kissed him deeply, and as they wrapped their arms around each other the pad in Danielle's hand dropped to the rugged floor. Casper was breathless at the way silk could accent a woman's body and make her feel so smooth. Between kisses they made their way over to the bed and lay down together.

On the floor the pad said, *"I cannot promise anything more, but I can promise you a night. I'll be in one of the guest rooms in the palace."*

The next morning Casper was awoken to someone shaking him, he opened his eyes slowly and realized the room was filled with sunlight. Immediately he jumped out of bed in search of his pants.

"Holy Moses what time is it?" he asked.

"Eight-thirty." Casper whirled around to face the voice as it wasn't at all the voice he was expecting. Ensign Freddy Maddox stood across the bed from him smiling.

"Freddy?? What are you doing here? Where's…" Casper stopped, probably not a good idea to announce whom he had spent the night with.

"Lt. Harper is getting the ship ready, sir. He told me to come get you from the palace," Freddy answered. "It's taken me twenty minutes to wake you up." Casper sighed, maybe last night wasn't such a good idea, considering how tired he felt now.

"Thanks Freddy…and the other ships how are they doing?" Casper was trying to very indiscreetly find out where it was Danielle had gotten to and when exactly she had left.

"All twenty-two ships are flight and combat ready save the *Spartan*," Freddy replied. Casper stopped getting dressed and looked at the ensign.

"What's wrong with the *Spartan*?" he asked. Silently he prayed it had nothing to do with the whereabouts of her captain.

"She's having some engine trouble. Commander Tyson was the first one on the pad trying to fix it with her engineers, she even brought over some of the experts from the other ships' engineering staff. I think she might be holding onto some of them during the mission just in case," Freddy answered. Little did Freddy know his little explanation had Casper's heart going ninety miles an hour. Engine trouble? Experts? Danielle undoubtedly made a staffing change putting Isis on her ship instead of his. Casper looked to his side…she was *good.*

"Oh?" Casper replied as if it didn't matter. "Did you bring me a list of names that were switched around?" he asked seemingly unconcerned. Freddy reached into his uniform pocket and pulled out a com pad.

"I did; in fact, Lt. Harper told me too, he seemed really weird when he gave it to me," Freddy said.

"How so?" Casper asked as he took the pad.

"Well, he had this kind of…ridiculously stupid goofy grin on his face," Freddy replied. Casper sighed and knew what that meant immediately. He looked down at the list of crewmen switched from other ships to the *Spartan* and sure enough, halfway down the list he saw Isis' name in bright glowing letters.

"Shit," Casper breathed.

"There a problem, Captain?" Freddy asked. Casper shook his head in vexation.

"You don't have a gun on hand do you, Fred?" he asked.

"Uh…no why sir?"

"I think I want to end it a bit faster than expected," Casper joked. Once again his morbid humor was received by a horrified look and a pale face. "Oh for the love of…lighten up, Freddy, it was a joke…forget it. Come on, let's get to the launch before everyone leaves without us."

They were climbing aboard a transport car when Patricia and Anthony came up to them. Patricia, face wet with tears, smiled as best she could.

"Promise me I'll hear from you again," she whispered. Casper pulled her into a hug.

"As much as possible, Mom, I love you," he replied. To his father he shook hands and saluted when the man saluted first.

"You're a proud man, Casper, and I'm proud of you," he said. Casper gave a nod and with that, the transport door closed and they were off to the launch. Along the streets signs that had been "welcome home" only a day ago now read "good luck" and "god speed." It was touching to know his people were behind him one hundred percent.

When they reached the command central Casper knew he'd have to prepare himself for the looks of sadness he was going to get. Standing at the entrance behind which were six of his ships including the *Specter* and *Spartan* Casper took a deep breath, fixed his uniform, and walked in as if nothing was wrong.

The moment he stepped onto the pad he felt eyes whirl around to look at him and yet every time he turned to look the individuals would suddenly be very interested in what they were doing. Finally he arrived at the *Spartan* that was docked just beside the *Specter*. He decided to see what the engine problems were about and headed inside.

He heard her voice, before he even got through the doors to engineering.

"*I don't care if you get vertigo, get up there and attach that relay!! And you!! stop dicking around and start doing some real work!! so help me if I find you slacking one more time I…* what's that?…*no you cannot have a break to go to the bathroom piss yourself if you have to, get back to work!!*" Casper had to laugh, he stood on the balcony that looked over the main engine room where it looked like Danielle had her soldiers running around at warp speed. The comic thought came to him that maybe if the engine was filled with the engineers under Danielle's command the ship would go faster then if the actual engine was working.

"Captain on deck!!" Casper didn't know which of the panicked engineers had time to notice him standing there but the one man was all it took. Everyone froze where they stood and snapped to attention. From where she stood down below Danielle looked up and finally caught sight of him.

"Thank you, at ease," Casper waved. He barely finished speaking before everyone stepped it into turbo again and started whizzing around to their duties. Danielle, however, climbed the ladder to stand beside him. Casper held out the pad of names.

"You want to tell me what this is about?" he asked. She looked at it and smiled.

"It's a list of highly trained personnel needed to get this ship running," she replied.

"I couldn't help but notice Ensign Soul is one of the few engineers transferred to your permanent roster," Casper stated. Danielle raised a provocative eyebrow and smiled.

"I've got her working on some highly volatile chemical coolant underneath some dangerously sharp metal siding," she said. Casper's mouth dropped open and he paled, and Danielle burst out laughing. "It was a joke, Casper…but the look on your face was priceless!"

"So why do you need her here?" he asked.

"Oh geez, Casper not everything is about you. My ship honestly needs the best personnel working on her right now to get her going; Soul is one of the best, your own engineer recommended her," Danielle explained. It was a believable explanation and Casper knew he was getting too worked up so he nodded with a smile.

"Play nice," he said.

"Unlike last night, hmm?" Danielle quipped as he turned to leave. He turned around quickly to see if anyone else had heard her comment but fortunately no one had and she was already gone down the ladder screaming at some defenseless ensign who was using a wrong tool.

Casper was walking down the hall from engineering when suddenly a supply door opened and he was pulled inside. The room was barely big enough for the two of them and dimly lit. Casper could barely make out Isis' face.

"I was worried about you last night, where were you?" Isis asked. Casper cleared his throat and swallowed hard trying not to let the truth out because he still didn't know how he felt.

"I needed some time to think," he responded. Neglecting to add, *with my second in command*. He felt Isis' hand gently rub his arm in support.

"I can't believe this is happening to you, it's just so unfair," she said. Casper could hear her voice shake slightly and took her into his arms.

"I know, but I'm trying not to concentrate on the end but rather the task at hand. I want to get Atkinson before I depart this world. I want him to know the suffering I have," Casper replied.

"I can understand that," Isis sighed. "I wish I hadn't been put on the *Spartan*, I wanted to be closer to you." Casper again found it hard to keep his concentration, this time not because of the question but because of the small room and Isis' proximity to him.

"We all have to do our duties, even if that does separate us, but there'll be transports between ships, meetings between staff, this isn't goodbye," Casper said. Then he sighed and added, "yet."

"Don't talk like that please," Isis sniffed. In the soft light of the closet he saw a sparkle of a tear slide down her cheek. Casper gently took her face in his hands and wiped away the tear causing them to make direct eye contact.

"I know it's hard to face the facts but…" Casper never got to finish, Isis pressed against him and pressed her lips against his. When they broke for air Casper took a deep breath, "We need to get back to work, we shouldn't…" Again her body pressed up against his silenced him, she was really, *really* working him.

"Tyson's a slave driver, but she won't miss one engineer for ten minutes," Isis said breathlessly. She kissed his neck and he felt her start to undo the collar to his uniform, "Make that fifteen," she giggled. Casper knew he had to stop the madness, he shouldn't be doing this especially after what he had done with Danielle the night before. He owed Isis the truth.

"Isis stop," Casper sighed. And she did, she stopped cold.

"Yes?" she asked.

"There's something I need to tell you," Casper began.

"You and Tyson last night? I know about it," Isis replied. Casper was stunned beyond belief. It seemed to be a theme to shock the crap out of a dying man.

"You do??" he said incredulously.

"She approached me this morning and told me. I thought I'd be mad, but then she explained her feelings for you. She's a very intelligent woman, she explained that it was just a night and anything more than that was up to you, but if she knew you and I had something she wouldn't encroach on our territory," Isis explained. Casper's mind was doing a double take and going for a ride.

"You aren't mad?" he asked. "What I did was wrong I know that now I…"

"Casper, it's your decision to make, her or me, we both are at the understanding that we won't lose sleep over either decision, but neither of us wants to be with a man who's thinking of another woman," Isis admitted.

"Wow." Casper sighed. "I wish I could say one way or the other but with everything that's going on and...well me dying and all, I've kind of enjoyed the attention."

"Casper, don't talk about your death like no one will miss you." The sadness had returned to Isis' voice as had the tears. "I don't care who you choose, but I still care for you and I don't want you to die."

"Isis, I'm sorry, humor is my defense mechanism," Casper admitted. "Don't cry, sweetheart, please, I can't have people close to me breaking down. I need you to be strong, help me, help you be strong." With that Isis pressed herself against him once again and kissed him.

"Be with me now," she whispered. "Live each moment as just that." Casper was shocked she had taken the news of Danielle and him so well, especially after it had come from the other woman and not him. Once again, she continued undoing his uniform and kissing his neck.

"We've only got twelve minutes left." She laughed.

Minutes before launch Casper stood in his ready room looking out the window at the other ships on the pad. Word had been passed along that the *Spartan* was finally sea worthy but she'd be keeping her experts in case of any problems. He couldn't believe those women, they were both very forward, take-what-they-want and don't-cry-over-a-loss women, qualities he greatly admired in them. At the same time it made concentrating on the task at hand very, very difficult.

Harper came in the ready room and wiggled his eyebrows.

"So, king of kings, how'd it go last night?" he asked.

"Harper..." Casper drew out.

"Right, sorry, I just came to say all ships are prepped and ready to launch on your command," Harper said. Casper nodded and followed his friend out to the bridge where he took his rightful seat.

"Ensign Park, open a channel to all ships," Casper ordered.

"Link established, sir," Linda replied moments later. Casper took a deep breath. How was he supposed to thank so many men and women for joining him on a mission that had a higher fail percentage than a successful one?

"This is Captain Hawk to all ships…words cannot express my gratitude at what you are willing to do for me right now. We have fought together valiantly and triumphantly. Though this will probably be my last hurrah, I'd like to believe you will all keep on fighting as the family I have come to see in you. Truly from the grunts to the officers I thank each and everyone of you for following me today and know that when the time comes I shall continue to be with you in spirit and guide you in times of need. Okay, form up in gamma formation on the far side of Luna Three, further flight info will be given at that time. Hawk out." When the line was cut Casper slouched back down into his chair and rubbed his temples, he was so tired and his body was starting to ache.

"Sir, I have something I'd like you to look at on your station," Harper said. Casper looked at his armory officer and wondered what it was he needed to do now. Then he turned to his panel and spoke,

"Send it over, Lieutenant," he replied. After a few moments a message began to dance across the main screen. It read: *It's five hours until we reach Luna Three, I doubt anything will happen from here to there. Why don't you use this time to rest, there's no point in getting all the way there and not being able to do anything. I can take the bridge until then... Harp.*

Harper had discreetly sent the message over the panel so Casper wouldn't look weak or like he was being babied by his friends. It was a courtesy Casper appreciated very much and he looked up at Harper with a smile.

"It looks good, Lieutenant, but I think I'm going to compare it with other documents in my quarters…you have the bridge," Casper said. With a nod and a smile shared between the two Casper headed off to his quarters for some rest.

When he got to his room he stripped to his skivvies and lay down welcoming the comfort and warmth of the bed. As he started to drift off into a gentle sleep his thoughts were of his home and his simple yet complicated childhood. A life that seemed ages ago and a way he would never again know.

Casper ran down the hall of the palace to his parents' room, he was five years old today and very excited to start celebrating. However, in all his excitement for his birthday, he hadn't bothered to sit still while his nanny helped him into his finery for a party that would be held later that day leaving his small prince uniform a disheveled mess.

"Mommy, Mommy, Mommy, Mommy, Mommy, Mommy!" he squealed. He reached his parents' door just as it opened and two strong arms scooped him up off the floor.

"Hey there's the birthday boy, I could have sworn you were a herd of elephants!" Anthony smiled.

"No, Daddy, it's just me!!" Casper giggled. "I'm a whole hand today!"

"That you are." His father smiled. "And do you know what else that means?" Casper didn't know, he looked at his father confused. "It means you start schooling soon, are you ready to work hard?"

"I don't wanna work, I wanna play!" Casper squealed. There was still a lot he didn't understand at his age, but one thing he did was the difference between fun and not fun: work and play.

"Oh come now, Casper, you're a big boy now and a prince, you'll have many responsibilities when you grow big," Anthony said. Casper didn't like what he was hearing, he wanted to grow up, but he didn't want to have to work to get there.

"NO!!!" he screeched. "I wanna be a kid! No work! No work!" Anthony laughed and hugged his boy tighter close to his chest, somehow hearing his father's heartbeat calmed him down some.

"I'll be proud of you no matter what you do, Casper. You're a smart boy and I love you," he said.

"I love you too, Daddy…can we open presents now?" Casper asked.

"No, dorkus, that's not until after the party." Casper looked over his father's shoulder to his brother who stood in the doorway. Maverick's uniform was in somewhat better shape than his own, the white collar was done up, nothing was wrinkled, his shoes were shined and his belt buckle gleamed. Casper looked at his own uniform and felt slightly less important than his older brother, who was a full three years older and suddenly felt the urge to look just as good.

Just then Patricia came out of the bathroom in her beautiful royal gown. Casper struggled free of his father's arms and ran up to her clutching her leg.

"Mommy, fix it so I look better than him!" Casper said, pointing to Maverick. Patricia laughed and knelt down to fix Casper's outfit.

"Are you excited for your special day?" she asked. Casper beamed and nodded happily.

"Daddy says I have to go to school now, but I don't wanna," he said.

"But, sweetheart, you're a big boy now; besides, don't you want to learn what your brother has?" Patricia asked. Casper looked over to Maverick who stuck out his tongue and made a face then turned back to his mother.

"I'm gonna learn more than him, and I'm gonna be the bestest there ever was! Even better than Mav!" Casper announced. Patricia smiled and stood as she finished fixing his uniform and took his hands.

"Are you boys ready to meet some very important people?" Patricia asked. Casper and Maverick nodded.

"Best behaviors, hmm boys?" Anthony asked. Again Casper and Maverick nodded happily as they started out the door.

"What if Casper does something dumb? Is he going to get thrown in jail?" Maverick asked. Casper didn't like it when his older brother belittled him and he had had enough. It was his birthday and like his parents said, he was a big boy now and could defend himself. So as hard as he could Casper kicked Maverick in the shins and took off down the hallway screaming bloody murder.

"I'm gonna get you, you big doody head!" Maverick screeched. Casper laughed as he ran as hard as he could. He turned briefly to see if his brother had given chase but it proved to be to his own demise. What Casper hadn't realized what that he was headed straight into a large planter vase. With a large thwack and a crash both it and Casper sprawled out all over the floor.

Casper was dazed but when he sat up he realized he had ripped his nice dress pants and cut his knee. He was all happy seconds ago, and now he was dirty and his knee hurt. After a few restrained sniffs Casper burst into tears right on the spot.

Moments later Patricia scooped him up and rocked him gently to quiet him down.

"It's okay little one, mommy's got you, I'll always be here when you fall," she whispered. Then quietly she began to hum to Casper to comfort him like she always did when he scraped his knee. As she rocked him, Casper gently started to drift off in his mother's arms. "My brave little prince, I'll always open my arms to you." Her words were as soft as her skin, soon Casper was fast asleep.

He woke up, in his bed, much, much older. Suddenly he felt chills and needed to get warm. Casper got up his body aching with cold and headed over to the shower and turned the water on as hot as his skin could take it. Standing under the hot water soothed his aching body but not the ache in his heart. He knew what was happening to him. It wasn't just the chills, it was the beginning of the end. The water dripped off the tip of his long hair and down his back, in front it dripped off his nose as he leaned against the wall letting the water fall where gravity took it.

An alert drew his attention and he turned off the water with a sigh and pressed the com panel just outside the shower.

"Hawk here," he answered.

"Captain, your presence is requested on the bridge."

"Have we reached Luna Three?" he asked.

"No, sir…um…the lieutenant says it's important." Casper rolled his eyes and sighed.

"Okay I'll be there in a moment," he replied. He got out of the shower and pulled on his uniform.

After he was dressed he made his way toward the bridge, when he got there Harper was kicked back in the captain's chair.

"What's the emergency?" Casper asked. Harper turned around and raised an eyebrow.

"Tell me you gave orders that I didn't know about?" he asked.

"Noooo…why?" Casper asked cautiously. Harper shook his head and pointed to the view screen.

"Well because we're fifteen minutes from Luna Three but one of your ships just broke away and jumped into deep space," he said. Casper's eyes bugged wide open, and he looked at the formation of ships on his sensor. They were in fact minus one ship.

"Who was it and why did they go?" Casper asked, quite upset that one of his ships would choose now to go rogue.

"The *Spartan.* I am still trying to get a hold of them to ask them why," Harper replied. Casper smacked his forehead and shook his head.

"Why is she doing this to me?" he muttered. Harper looked at him and snorted a laugh.

"In her defense she *was* having engine trouble to begin with," he offered.

"Sir, I think I've got something," Linda said from the com panel. "It's a weak message, but it's them alright."

"Put it through," Casper said. The screen was very fuzzy and Casper could barely make out Danielle's second in command on the screen.

"…aptain Hawk, we eem…have passed through…rip in space. We aren't…ure where…are…ight now…systems are failing…'re dead in space…Repeat…you get this…sage we…being hurled…some kind…space rip…require…diate aid…" The message cut out and was gone, Casper looked at Linda who shrugged.

"That's it, sir, nothing else," she said.

"Crap, both of them on one ship," Casper mumbled to himself. "Alright…track them Freddy as best you can and…"

"Sir, we're being hailed by the *Liberator,*" Linda said. Casper nodded and she put them through. Captain Huron appeared on the screen leaning in and looking very serious.

"Captain Hawk, I'm nominating my ship to go after the *Spartan*, I say this with the utmost respect but you don't really have mass amounts of time to find both Atkinson and the *Spartan*. We'll catch up with you when we get them," Huron said. Casper rubbed his temples, his head was starting to hurt. He looked over to Harper who looked like he was agreeing with Huron.

"Take two ships with you and get back with us as fast as you can, we'll hold here as long as possible. We need to try and trace the fundamentalists anyway," Casper said.

"Back in a flash," Huron smiled. The communication was cut and the *Liberator* peeled out of formation with two ships following her then within seconds the ships jumped to deep space.

CHAPTER SIX

Several hours later Casper was sitting in his ready room going over star charts and trying to compare his position when he was abducted to where they were at the moment and where enemy space was. The squadron had been orbiting Luna Three for some time now waiting for the *Liberator* and the others to return so as to venture deeper into space together.

Finally Casper grew tired of the star charts and decided since they were at a lull he'd contact home while they were still in visual range. He made the communication and waited for someone to reply. After a few seconds his father's face appeared, Casper smiled.

"Hey pops, I know I haven't been gone all that long but…"

"I was expecting you to call sooner," Anthony joked. Casper laughed and shook his head.

"How's mom?"

"Scared, sad, depressed, and she's become a leech." Casper raised an eyebrow and narrowed an eye.

"Pardon?" he half laughed.

"The doctors, she's refusing to let them leave the lab with out a cure for you." Anthony sighed.

"Are they making any progress?" Casper asked. He knew it was an empty question because he knew the answer. He could see the despair and sadness in his father's eyes at the question so he smiled. "It's okay, Dad, I didn't really expect anything anyway." His father nodded, clearly not wanting to talk more about his son's mortality.

"And you? How is your mission going?" he asked.

"Actually we're still orbiting Luna Three, the *Spartan* had some engine trouble and I think her hyper drive kicked in and she disappeared on us…we're waiting for the *Liberator*, *Aquanaut,* and the *Hazard* to come back with her…Hey, Dad?" Casper asked.

"Yes?" Anthony asked.

"How's Maverick?" he asked. Anthony raised his eyebrows and let out a heavy sigh.

"Well…" Casper could see his father put his hands on the camera and turn it slightly to the left. It let Casper see his brother who was sitting out on one of the balconies with a blanket wrapped around his shoulders. Maverick seemed to be staring off into space barely moving or even blinking, just sitting and staring. Anthony then turned the camera back so Casper was looking at his father again. "He's been like that since you left. When he woke up and you were gone he shut down emotionally, he's barely saying a word. The doctor's got him on medication for depression," Anthony admitted. Casper sighed and looked away for a second then back again.

"Can you get him to come say hello?" he asked.

"I can get him to come here but saying anything is another matter," Anthony replied.

"Thanks Dad, and I love you." Casper smiled. His father smiled and nodded, not really able to reply due to the overwhelming emotion. Anthony disappeared off screen and moments later Maverick sat down with help from a guided hand, blanket still wrapped around his shoulders. Maverick's face was pale and impassive, his skin looked several shades lighter then it usually was. One thing was for sure, the man on the screen was not the strong-willed man Casper once knew.

"Hey, Mav, how are you?" Casper asked. Maverick simply shrugged. "What did you do today?"

"Sat," Maverick said plainly.

"I'm sorry I didn't say goodbye, I woke up late and we were having problems with the *Spartan* so I didn't really have time to…"

"Why did you go?" Casper was caught unawares.

"I need to find Atkinson, Mav, I can't let him get away with what he did to us," he replied. "Would you rather I stayed so you could watch me slowly die?"

"I'd rather you sent the rest of the squadron and stayed here with me," Maverick replied. Casper sighed and shook his head.

"I couldn't have done that and you know it," he said. Then he realized Maverick was the last man he wanted to get into a fight with.

"'Member how we used to fight when we were kids?" Casper asked, recalling his dream. Maverick nodded. "I was always jealous that you had three years on me, you always could dress yourself better, speak better and get everyone's attention…Man, you had everything and I hated you for it. Now, I realize I learned a lot from how you carried yourself back then, I owe you a lot, Mav." Maverick looked away from the screen and then back, not really replying to Casper's words. Clearly his brother was in shock and still didn't really know what to say. "It will be alright, Maverick, you're a strong guy and my big brother."

"Do you really believe it will all be okay?" Maverick asked.

"Yes, I do," Casper replied. "I can't imagine what they made you watch, but I'll tell you this, it's over now and you can get on with your life."

"While waiting for you to die," Maverick said coldly. Casper looked at his brother, holding his emotionless eyes.

"If that's what's got you in this funk, Mav, write me off," he said. Finally Casper got a reaction from his brother as Maverick's eyes got slightly larger.

"Write you off?" he asked. Casper nodded in response.

"If that's what it takes to make you get back to normal," he said.

"Casper, you say you were envious of what I could do and maybe there was a time that was right. Now, you have nothing to look up to, I failed you as an older brother and as any sort of a role model. *You're* the strong one, *you're* the one to be looked up to…I'm nothing, not now not ever," Maverick said. He lowered his head looking down at his hands as if he had lost his sense of adulthood.

"Mav, don't feed me a sob story that you're nothing; that's crap and you know it. Just because you don't do so well in physical battles doesn't mean you're any less of a man. In a political arena you can talk the devil into retiring and turning hell into a giant patio for God. Myself on the other hand, one whiff of diplomacy and I wet my pants and look for the nearest gun. Seriously all I can do is blow shit up," Casper replied. Maverick's face slowly cracked and a very tired, pathetic half smile appeared on his face. "Good heavens is that a smile?"

"Don't get used to it, it hurt my face," Maverick replied. Casper threw his hands in the air and smiled.

"Sweet Jesus he's got a sense of humor!!" he exclaimed. This drew a slight chuckle from Casper's brother and it made him feel better.

"Seriously, Casper, come home soon, don't stay away until…well the end," Maverick said quietly. Casper smiled gently and nodded.

"I'll try, Mav, really I will try," he said. "Tell Mom I love her and…I love you too, man." At this Maverick smiled again and shook his head.

"Oh you," he quipped. Casper was thrilled his brother was at least joking slightly with him. It showed the brother he knew was still inside the weakened shell of a man Maverick had become since they broke free.

"I'll talk to you again," he said. Maverick nodded and said his goodbyes.

Moments after Casper closed the com window a buzz at his desk got his attention.

"Captain Hawk here," he replied.

"Sir, the *Liberator*, *Aquanaut,* and *Hazard* have returned."

"Do they have the *Spartan*?" he asked.

"Yes, sir."

"How is she?"

"Pretty banged up, sir, com is down, engines are down but all life signs are accounted for."

"Okay, I'm on my way."

Casper left his ready room and took his place in his chair, then turned to Freddy.

"Bring it up on the monitor," he ordered. The screen flashed and then showed the three ships of his fleet all with tow cables extended. They moved slowly but when they finally moved out of view Casper sucked in a deep breath at the sight of the *Spartan*. The entire bridge crew seemed shocked at her appearance.

The ship looked like it had just come from a junk yard, pieces of its hull were missing or scorched, the lights flickered on and off. It looked dead, Casper could only imagine what her crew looked like.

"Sir, she's managed to bring com online," Linda said.

"Good, bring it up," Casper said. The screen was fuzzy but with some tweaking the picture became slightly better but the sound was still tunneled. Sitting in the captain's chair was a very weary looking second officer Tara Pratt. Casper's heart sank as Danielle appeared to be nowhere inside.

Tara's hair was out of place and her face was dirtied with soot, behind her several fires were being tackled by the crew.

"Lt. Pratt, what's the situation?" Casper asked.

"Sir, due respect, I couldn't begin to tell you if I tried, I just got here myself," she said.

"Just got there? Where's Commander Tyson?" Casper asked. Tara twisted in her seat and looked around the bridge.

"Hey any of you seen the commander?" she asked the people around. After a pause she turned back to the screen and shrugged. "Sorry, sir, everything happened too suddenly; we were seconds away from being ripped to space dust when we finally shut down the engine...well...it overloaded actually and crapped out...uh...exploded."

"Okay Lt., it's alright, I need you to find the commander for me and tell her I want to speak to her. I also want an injury report and damage, until then, make sure your people are all in one piece," he said. Tara smiled clearly grateful at Casper's easy attitude about everything.

"Thank you, sir," she said. "I'll do my best to…" Tara was cut off when a crewman came into view and spoke quietly into her ear. When the crewman disappeared Tara turned back to the screen and stood up. "Sorry, sir, I'm required elsewhere."

"What's going on, Lieutenant?" Casper asked.

"Fuel leak, vapor leak, life support on D-level is failing, the infirmary is destroyed…shit and I just got word that half the starboard docking bay door is seconds away from sucking twenty-eight people out into space. I'm a technician, sir, really I have to go so if there is nothing else…" Tara said.

"I understand, but I'd like you to dock with the *Specter* so we can help you out okay?" Casper asked.

"I don't know what condition the clamps are in but will give'er as best we can," Tara said. With that she disappeared from view and the line was cut. Casper sat back in his chair. The two women he cared for were on that ship and he had no idea if they were alright or not. This was definitely not helping his short life span any.

Moments later the two ships floated side by side, the rest of the squadron forming a protective barrier around them. Casper made his way down to the docking port. In another communication sent almost immediately after the first, he had told them to send over all their injured personnel. After that he and Harper had gone down to see just how many injured there were…there were a lot, much more than Casper had expected actually.

"Oh no…Casper look," Harper sighed. Casper who had been watching people run in and out of the space port carrying injured spun around to look at what Harper had found.

"There go a few more days…" Casper mumbled to himself. Gently being maneuvered through the port was Isis on a stretcher, she was conscious but her arm was coddled close to her body. Casper walked up to her and looked down at her.

"How bad?" he asked.

"The ship is junk. I'm surprised anyone made it," Isis hissed through the pain.

"I meant you," Casper smiled. Isis gave a short laugh and a cough.

"I was out for a few moments, I wake up and I'm being carried off. My lungs hurt, my arm, other than that, ten fingers, ten toes, I'm good," she replied. Casper nodded and gave her good hand a squeeze before letting her be carried off to the infirmary. Finally Lt Pratt, frazzled looking but still well in charge came through the space port on her own power.

"Sir, I can't thank you enough for taking the injured," Tara breathed.

"It's nothing, my duty as a squad leader," Casper said. Tara nodded and turned to watch the injured being moved with Harper and Casper.

"We didn't know what hit us, the engine kind of hiccupped but then we just…started going faster than I thought possible for our ship. The helmsmen were ill prepared, the engine room had no clue, we were tumbling head over tail for a good several minutes before it stopped," she explained. Casper wondered what could have possibly happened with their engines that caused such a reaction in the deep space jumper.

"Harper, get Maddox to run a systematic check on the area of space the *Spartan* was flying before she went haywire," Casper ordered. Harper nodded and took off down the hall, then Casper turned back to Tara. "Where's the commander?" He had been trying to hold off on the question so as not to seem too one-track minded but he couldn't do it any longer. Tara looked up at him away from the victims and, in fact, turned her whole body to him.

"If I knew, sir, she'd be here talking to you instead of me. I was just about to go loo…" Tara was cut off when one of the engineering crew rushed passed them, grabbed something off the *Specte*r and headed back. Casper managed to grab him before he disappeared again to ask what was going on.

"There's people still trapped on D-deck," he replied. Revealing the blowtorch he had picked up. "If we don't get them out of there within the next ten minutes there'll be a lot of letters to write home."

"Do you know if Commander Tyson is there?" Casper asked.

"I don't know, I think…someone might have said something but…please, sir, I have to go." Casper released the man but followed after him. As he ran behind the young man he went over the schematics of the *Spartan* in his head. The mess hall was on D-deck, all those people who had been caught unaware, Danielle must have been sitting down to lunch when it happened.

Casper had been dead on as they reached the mess hall doors and three engineers were working on using blow torches to open the door. The air in that area was already starting to get slightly stale indicating a lack of air flow.

"*There*!! PULL!!" one of the technicians yelled. Casper leaned in to help himself and with a lot of grunting and groaning they managed to open the mess hall doors.

"Get everyone out!" Casper ordered. The soldiers didn't have to be told twice; they were already herding people out in droves.

"Sir!" one soldier said. "The commander was in her private dining room!" Casper nodded and ran into the mess hall straight for the captain's mess. The door was partially open, someone had been trying to get in there but had obviously abandoned it when they had been set free from the mess hall. Casper didn't blame whomever it was, but he was glad someone had tried.

Again putting his effort into it and starting to get a little light headed because of the stale air, Casper pried the door open. It didn't take a second to find her, Danielle must have been standing when everything happened. She was in the corner of the room with the table and other junk nearly burying her from view. Casper rushed to her and started flinging things off her. When he got to the table, however, it was too heavy for him. Just when he was going to stop to get some help Harper appeared beside him.

"You shouldn't be here, it's too dangerous," Casper grunted as they tried to lift together.

"I promised your parents, that and she's my friend too," Harper groaned back. Finally they removed the table and pushed it aside. Casper was now able to get a better look at Danielle, half her face was covered in blood that had seeped into her uniform collar and she looked quite pale.

"Dani, come on give me something," Casper urged. He was sweating hard, it was dripping off his face and his breathing was becoming much more labored. Harper was the same, as he leaned against the wall to catch his breath.

"We…gotta…get…out…of…here," Harper breathed. Casper nodded, he started to lift Danielle into his arms but was overcome with dizziness.

"I…can't…do it," he breathed. Harper came over and tried as well but it was no luck, neither of them had the energy. They were losing oxygen too fast.

"You three need some air?" Casper and Harper turned to see four people in pressure suits led by Lt. Pratt. Casper smiled and nodded and they were soon given portable air filters. It wasn't fresh air, but it gave them enough air to get out of there. Danielle was lifted onto a stretcher and carried out.

When they were off D-deck and Pratt had taken off the top half of her pressure suit they watched Danielle get carried away to the infirmary.

"You two were lucky, sir, life support cut out five minutes ago. I'm amazed you were still conscious," she said.

"You can do amazing things when a life is on the line, Lt, never forget that," Casper smiled. Tara just shook her head in amazement, then she looked back to Casper.

"Sir, are you alright? You still look really pale, and Harper's color has already returned to him," she asked. Harper put a hand on Casper's shoulder and turned to look at him.

"She's right, how do you feel?" he asked. Truth was, Casper had never really gotten enough air into his lungs and was feeling rather sick.

"I'll be fine, I just need some more air," he rasped.

"Bullshit you are," Harper deadpanned.

"Alright, you called it…" Casper couldn't stop the room from spinning. He suddenly felt numb all over his body. His legs just didn't want to support him anymore.

"We need another stretcher over here!" Tara's voice was distant and tunneled, it was like she was a thousand miles away. Casper gave in to the darkness like he had several times in the past couple days and slumped to the floor.

"Dear, you are fifteen years old, I don't care how much you don't want to do it, you have to. It's your duty as Prince of Hearth Condes."

"Second Prince," Casper corrected his mother. Maverick, his father and mother were dressed in formal attire; there was a dinner in the family's honor being held in town by the people of the main city. Casper hated his choke collar uniform, and he hated being paraded around behind his brother like an idiot.

"Son, now's not the time to try and get out of this dinner, we all must be there," Anthony said. Casper rolled his eyes and turned down the hallway toward his room. As he walked he heard the distinct sound of Maverick's dress shoes jogging toward him. He turned just in time to have both his shoulders grabbed and get shoved into the wall hard, by his older, stronger brother.

"Back off, Mav," Casper hissed.

"Listen, you little puke, you are a prince like it or not, we have duties. I hate this uniform too, but if I have to suffer so do you. This dinner isn't just another ball put on by Mom and Dad, it's a gift from the people of this city who love them and us," Maverick said.

"My heart's breaking, can I go now?" Casper sighed.

"Cass, you're separating yourself from us, don't fight what you were born into," Maverick said.

"Nope sorry, not sold yet." Casper shrugged. Maverick shook his head.

"Then you leave me no choice…" his older brother said. Before Casper knew what was going on he was flipped on his stomach to the cold marble floor with his brother sitting on his back. Maverick grabbed his left leg and started to tug it back toward him.

"OW OW OW!! STOP!!!" Casper pained. One of these days he'd kick his brother's butt but today wasn't that day.

"Will you go?" Maverick asked.

"What??" Casper pained again. A sharp tug made him flinch and cry out in pain.

"Are you going to go?" Maverick asked again.

"ALRIGHT! *Alright, I'll go, I'll go*!!!" Casper screamed. His brother let him go only to grab his shirt collar and drag him down the hall to Casper's room. Maverick dragged him inside and tossed his uniform at him.

"If you're not out and ready to go in five minutes I'm coming in here and kicking your ass, are we clear?" he asked.

"Yes, sheesh," Casper sighed. He believed that his brother would do it too, so he got dressed as quickly as possible and headed outside. At the palace gates his family was waiting for him, his mother with a bright smile on her face.

"I'm glad you decided to join us," she said.

"Cause I had a choice," Casper mumbled, to which Maverick pinched his arm as hard as humanly possible. "OOOOOW!!!" Casper whined.

"Now that we're on our way I can tell you something very important, Casper," Anthony said. Angry though he might have been Casper was still curious.

"What?" he asked. His father reached into his pocket and pulled out a small box and handed it to him. Casper opened it and looked inside. The box held a small golden pin. Curious still, Casper took it out and looked closely at it. It had military insignia on it and the family crest. "What is it?" Casper asked, looking at his father.

"Son, you're a wild spirit and your mother and I have recognized that and we want to give you a choice," Anthony said. Casper raised an eyebrow and looked at Maverick who just smiled. He looked back to his parents expectantly.

"What's going on?" he asked.

"Well, next year you turn sixteen, you'll be an adult then and so instead of sitting around the palace following your brother around as he learns the ways of the counsel, we're giving you the option of going military. An option that would one day put you in charge of the entire Hearth Zebra Centaury squadron," Patricia explained. Casper looked at the pin in his hand, he had heard stories of the tough military that would come and go from the landing pads outside the city. At many of his parents' dinners there would be a man or woman dressed in military uniform looking really cool with the crystal blade tucked neatly at their sides.

"For real?" Casper asked. He could just see himself in charge of a squadron of ships sitting on the bridge of a ship fighting for peace. Often he'd stand on the western balcony of the palace where he could see the ships were taking off for another eight months and always thought they looked so majestic and proud. The ships made little noise as they cut through the air and disappeared through the clouds. Oh how Casper wanted to know where they were going, and now, he was being given that option.

"For real, son, your mother and I have decided that she'll pass the reigns of home security and politics on to your brother, and I will pass on the military way of life to you." Anthony smiled. Casper couldn't stop the smile from creeping across his face. He looked at Maverick who nodded "congrats." Then he turned back to his parents and flew across the seat pulling them both into a hug.

"This is so COOL!!" he exclaimed. "Oh man! Thank you soooooo much!!!" Anthony laughed, but then looked at Casper seriously when he sat back down.

"The military is not as glamorous or fun as it may seem to you now, Casper. Sometimes you have to make life and death choices, you have to be willing to sacrifice a lot and work even harder. It is *a lot* of work, son. Are you going to be willing to do that?" he asked. Casper sat up straighter in his seat, he wanted to seem mature and all knowing at the moment. There was no way he'd blow an opportunity like this!

"I can do it, Dad, and I'll be so good at it everyone will remember me as the greatest leader there ever was!" Casper exclaimed. Maverick knuckled him in the rib cage.

"Second, don't forget, I'll still have seniority over you," he said.

"Whatever, meathead," he shot back. He looked back at the pin and smiled.

"This is so friggin' cool," he said. The smile never left his face that whole night, especially after dinner when the news was announced to the whole room. Even Maverick stood and clapped for Casper which made it seem so much more important.

As they were leaving Anthony approached Casper with a young woman standing beside him.

"Casper, this is Danielle Tyson," Anthony introduced. "She's going to be going through training with you and Sean-Patrick."

"*Harper's joining too*????" Casper screeched. He hadn't meant to sound like such a small child but having his best friend training with him for possibly the coolest job ever was exciting.

"Yes, he is," Anthony laughed. "Now Danielle's family are good friends of ours. They are also very high up in the counsel, so I want you two to be friends okay? Say goodbye and I'll say goodbye to her parents." Anthony walked off leaving Casper alone with Danielle, a rather pretty girl with really long hair.

"Do you ever trip on that?" Casper asked.

"What?"

"Your hair, does it ever get in your way?" he repeated. Danielle reached behind her and pulled some of her strawberry blonde locks forward.

"Not really, but it's good for strangling annoying little weak punks like you!" she snarled. Casper was stunned and slightly intimidated by the tall girl who seemed so nice only moments ago.

"Wh, what?" Casper swallowed. Danielle started laughing and shook her head.

"Poor gullible prince, I'm going to have to keep an eye on you," she snorted.

"Hey! I'm going to be your boss someday! How old are you anyway?" he shot back.

"Sixteen stupid, a year older than you. I should have joined up this year, but my parents wanted me to wait until *you* came along. Sometimes I think they want me to baby-sit you." Danielle sighed. Casper was getting furious with this girl, who did she think she was??

"You're nothing but a know-it-all! You probably won't even

make it through training, none of the girls will, you're all to weak. Why don't you drop out now and go cook something?" he growled. Danielle's face curled into a wicked smile.

"Actually the cooking's done, wanna know what I made?" she asked. He wasn't expecting that response from her and didn't know what to say.

"Uh, okay…" he said.

"*A knuckle sandwich*!!!" Then POW! Casper was knocked flat on his butt with a freshly bruised face. He rubbed his cheek as he watched the sadistic girl jog off to catch up to her family. Maverick, who had been watching the whole ordeal came over with a goofy smirk on his face. Casper thought his brother was coming to rub it in, but instead in a surprise move Maverick helped him to his feet.

"Don't worry, I won't tell anyone you got decked by a girl." He smiled. "We royal brothers have to stick together." Even though he appreciated his brother's kindness, he still didn't like the fact that Danielle had punched him. He frowned all the way back to the transport car. When he got in his mother looked at him in shock.

"Did that little harlot do that to you? I'm going to talk to her parents next time I see her. I swear they have no control…"

"Mom, it's okay really, you don't have to," Casper interrupted. "I deserved it anyway, I said chicks couldn't make it through basic." Patricia's face curled into a smile and she let out a laugh, then she shook her head.

"You did deserve it then." She sighed. "Oh poor thing, come here." Casper sat beside his mother who wrapped her arms around him, like many times before she began to hum and following that like all the other times, Casper began drifting off to sleep.

"My commando," he heard his father say.

"Don't call him that…not yet, he's still my little prince," his mother said. Casper snuggled closer to the protective arms of his mother and was comforted by the thought that he'd probably never see that Danielle after basic again.

"Up the O2 and get another injection of adrenaline."

"Another one? Doctor, he's had three."

"Don't question, not now, do."

"Yes, doctor." After a brief intermission in time Casper felt something press into his neck and suddenly he felt his heart jump to light speed. His eyes flew open and he gasped for air sitting straight up on the med bed.

"Welcome back to the living, Captain." The doctor smiled.

"How long have I been out?" Casper asked.

"Two hours, nothing more," she said. "If you'll excuse me." Casper nodded and the doctor rushed off to treat the many other patients that were in the infirmary. Everything came back to Casper, and he suddenly remembered the condition his friends had been in. He swung his legs over the edge of the bed and despite feeling a little woozy he stood.

"Easy there." Casper turned to see Isis coming up to him. Her face was cleaner now and her arm looked like it had healed nicely. "Just a sprain and some smoke, I'm good as new."

"I'm glad to hear that. Are you sure you're alright?" he asked. Isis smiled and took his arm so he wouldn't topple over.

"Better than you it seems," she replied. "I heard about your heroics. You helped save a lot of lives...including Commander Tyson's."

"I had to get them out before life support failed," Casper replied.

"That's why everyone loves you. I have to get back to work on *Spartan*, she took a beating but that bitch is tough. Will I see you later?" Isis asked.

"Senior staff will have a meeting at some point, including main engineers." He smiled. "You'd better be there." Isis nodded with a smile and disappeared from sick bay.

After watching her go Casper spun around and scanned sick bay but found no sign of Danielle. He grabbed a nearby medical technician and asked if they had any information.

"She's in a private room next door. Her crew insisted she have her privacy out of respect," the tech said. Casper nodded and headed next door. The room he entered was dark and quiet; it would be good for a recovering patient. Casper never ceased to be proud of his soldiers, they always showed the utmost respect for their superiors.

"Dani?" Casper asked quietly. The form on the bed opened her eyes slightly and then closed them.

"I'm awake," she said. Her voice was hoarse and quiet, but the important thing was she was coherent. Casper came up and gently sat on the bed beside her. Danielle sat up slightly and leaned on the wall then looked at Casper. "So what do we do now?" she asked.

"About what?" Casper asked.

"The *Spartan*, I don't need to see her to know it'll be at *least* two weeks before she's jump worthy, let alone the weeks it'll take to get her back up to par. She's space junk, Cass, we just need to decide if her crew will stay on Luna Three to wait for transport back to earth or we get dispersed to the other ships," Danielle hoarsed. She started to cough, so Casper handed her a glass of water which she accepted graciously.

"What do you think we should do?" he asked. She looked up at him and smiled.

"You're supposed to make these decisions remember, don't prey on the weak," she said. Casper had to laugh,

"You're one to talk!" he exclaimed. "Do you remember what happened the first time we met?" Danielle raised an eyebrow and shook her head. "You knocked me on my ass, flat out, you said you'd made a knuckle sandwich and BAM! I was in the dust." Danielle seemed to search her mind for the event and then recognition crossed her face and she burst out laughing.

"I had almost forgotten!" she snorted. "Oh the memories and look at us now."

"Yeah, look at us now." Casper's voice was sadder than he meant it to be, but it was how he felt. Instead of carefree teenagers Casper was weeks away from death and Danielle was recovering from some serious injuries. He looked away from her with embarrassment at the tears that threatened in his eyes. Just when he figured it was time to make his exit, he felt her hand on his. Casper looked at her despite the tears sliding down his cheek.

"It's okay to cry, you aren't invincible," she said softly. Casper wiped away the tears and leaned in to hug her tightly.

"I'm glad you're okay," he whispered into her neck.

"Takes a lot more than an overturned ship to stop me...besides, who'd baby-sit you if I wasn't around?" Danielle chided. Casper burst out laughing and looked her in the eye. Her face was bruised and dirty, but her eyes were clear and compassionate. He leaned in and kissed her. It was a long, simple, heartfelt, glad-to-be-alive kiss and then it ended.

"I need to figure out what I'm going to do with your ship," he said, still leaning forehead to forehead with her. She nodded but said nothing, she was still recovering from the kiss they just shared. After running his hand along her back he stood up and headed to the exit. He had *a lot* of work to do, and he didn't have time to think about personal issues just yet.

Casper decided he needed everyone's input on this one. He had called a meeting of all the ships' captains and first officers and chief engineers. There were too many people to fit into the *Specter's* operations room, so Casper had ordered them all into one of her cargo bays that had been cleared out and filled with chairs.

"Okay, you all are now fully apprised of the situation." Casper sighed. "We have two options: we keep going into deep space at light speed, or we trace back and go through the rip that the *Spartan* accidentally went through. Although, my hopes are we can get through it..."

"With out getting torn to pieces like the *Spartan*? Leaving us worm food?" Captain Jeffrey's second in command Lt. Merry jumped in. Captain Jeffrey, silently scolded his second in command then looked at Casper.

"Unfortunately, I'd have to agree with Merry, I don't think it's worth risking so many ships, especially the *Specter* for a half-assed plan," Jeffrey said. Across from him Captain Lexis stood up to get everyone's attention and to show the fact that he didn't approve of Jeffrey's opinion.

"That's why you aren't in command of this squadron," Lexis said, narrowing his eyes. "And why your opinion matters very little. If Captain Hawk thinks we can do it safely then I say we do it." There were different mumblings in the crowd none of which Casper could make out.

"I thought this *wasn't* a dictatorship," Jeffrey snapped. "I though he asked everyone's opinion on the matter, and I was simply stating mine."

"Still doesn't give you or your minion the right to talk like that, you can express your opinion but not in that manner," Lexis replied. This time Lt. Merry stood up not caring if he was outranked by almost half the room *or* captain Lexis.

"*MINION*??? How dare you!! I'll express myself however I damn well..." Merry never finished as Jeffrey yanked him back to his seat.

"Apologies, Captain Lexis, Lt. Merry is slightly anxious at the moment, actually all the time, he never was one to sit down," Jeffrey replied. The entire room let out a slight chuckle, but then turned back to the task at hand.

"Okay, captains, I'd like you to confer with your second in command and your engineer. I want to know if the ships can take a beating and keep flying and I also want to know if you think your crews are up for this," Casper replied. "Keep in mind this rip is probably how the fundamentalists have been sneaking into our territory for the past several years and would probably shorten our journey considerably. Dismissed." The group stood but milled around the room speaking with their staff. Casper, who had been standing for quite sometime now sat down and rubbed his temples. He was so tired and felt like all his energy had been sucked out of him. He had only been pushing it a little bit since he found out he was infected but already it seemed like any day now he'd never wake up.

"Still hanging in there?" Harper asked. Casper looked at him and knew he couldn't lie to the man.

"I'm tired, really tired, but I'm still going," he replied. Harper nodded and held out a mug of something steaming, on second smell, it was a nice hot cup of coffee. "You know me too well," Casper smiled as he accepted the mug. Harper gave a nod as they were joined by Casper's chief engineer Ryan Keeper, who sat down with the two and wiped some sweat off his forehead.

"I tried, Captain, I mean I really tried, myself and three other engineers of the squadron we gave it our all but…the *Spartan* is beyond repair, she needs an entire overhaul. She needs to be towed back to earth, all systems shut down, engine removed and replaced…and this ain't no small job she's wrecked pretty bad," Ryan sighed. Then he stretched his neck and cracked his back. "Forgive me I haven't slept since we left dock, since we started I've been shuttling back and forth between the *Specter* and the *Spartan* because or her problems. This is my first time sitting down," he admitted.

"I appreciate all the work you do Ryan," Casper smiled. "Now I have to ask you, we go back through that rip, are we going to end up like Tyson and her crew?" Ryan stretched back yet again and then leaned forward on the table.

"No," he replied. Casper looked at Harper then back to Ryan who was still looking at them.

"That's it? No? Flat out? You said it yourself the *Spartan* is junk," Casper said. "She was fine when we left dock."

"No, she wasn't…how much did Commander Tyson tell you about her ship captain? Due respect that ship shouldn't have left dock." Casper's brow crinkled menacingly slow and furiously.

"What…do…you…mean…she…shouldn't…have…left…space… Dock?" he asked in a low threatening angry voice. It was so intimidating Casper almost scared himself and some nearby officers who were listening. Ryan even seemed to move his chair back ever so slightly.

"Uh…I'm only saying that, she's an old ship, Captain, one of the oldest in the fleet. She was supposed to be undergoing an overhaul when you returned, and Tyson axed the project altogether," Ryan explained. Casper's head swirled with anger. He had been lied to and if he hadn't been with Danielle that night or with Isis, he would have been going over ships' records! They *knew* that and they abused his trust and feelings. Isis was one, but Danielle secured his total attention!

"They *used me*," Casper hissed. Harper looked at him and raised an eyebrow.

"You don't think Danielle…"

"She knew about Isis! She probably spoke to her about the ship…my *god* it was a total lie!" Casper gasped. Harper shook his head.

"No, they couldn't…they wouldn't be that deviant, they're good people," he said. Casper was breathing hard trying to calm himself down. He was livid at the moment and saw nothing but red.

"Sorry, gentlemen, but I'm confused," Ryan asked.

"Uh, best you don't know, Ry, why don't you take it easy for the next few hours we won't need you for a while," Harper said. Ryan smiled graciously and stood up.

"In that case I'll be in my quarters with a steak and then my bed," he said. "Goodnight, gents." Harper nodded and waved goodbye to the engineer and then turned to put a sturdy hand on Casper's arm.

"Cass, you need to relax, this can't be good for you," Harper soothed.

"They used me! Together they used me! It was all some sick…" Suddenly a wave of dizziness hit Casper, he sucked in a deep breath and lowered his head.

"Casper…you're bleeding," Harper said quietly. Casper looked up at him and then brought two fingers up to his nose, sure enough, his fingers came back into his sight slick with blood.

"What did I do to deserve such a life," Casper breathed. "Harp, I don't feel so good."

"Come on, man, let's get you out of this stuffy room," Harper replied. He went to stand but Casper grabbed his friend's arm and made him sit again.

"No, just run to the doc and get a shot of adrenaline, maybe some Kleenex while you're at it," Casper said. Harper seemed startled by the idea that Casper wasn't going to leave the proceedings.

"Cass, you can't…"

"I've been messed with enough today, Sean, I don't need you turning on me as well," Casper hissed quietly. "Now go." Harper frowned but nodded and was soon making his way out of the bay.

Casper wiped his nose on his sleeve so as not to appear obvious and then called the room back into order. Everyone sat down and looked at him awaiting further instructions.

"Kay, I'm not going to ask anyone to go through with this who doesn't want to. I totally understand if any of you want to back out now, but that's what I'm asking you to do. Anyone who has problems, leave now," Casper ordered. It was slightly uplifting to see the entire room sit perfectly still, clearly the engineers had told their captains what Ryan had told Casper about the rip.

"I'm glad you're all with me on this." He sighed. "Now because of its size we can only go through two at a time…"

"And the *Spartan*?" Tara asked. She was representing her ship all on her own as the engineers and commander were otherwise occupied. However, the mere mention of the ship upset Casper; he leaned over the table.

"Space trash, cut her up, blast her into oblivion, crash her into the moon surface, I don't give a damn. I've been informed *only now* that she wasn't fit to fly and yet she left Hearth Condes. Tell me, Lt. Pratt, did you know about her condition?" Casper growled. He didn't care if he was embarrassing her in front of the entire squadron, but he hoped the embarrassment would get back to those knowing of the situation.

Tara stood, she wasn't one to be intimidated, along with all the other females under his command.

"Sir, I did," she replied, without a hint of remorse. "And I'm not going to place the blame anywhere else. I was one of the individuals who said we could get her in the air, but I was not one of the ones who was a part of those chosen to keep it from you. Many of us on the *Spartan* have been on it for years and aren't ready to get left behind on such an important mission."

"Lt. Pratt, I'm relieving the entire command crew of the *Spartan* and condemning the ship. As for her crew, they'll be dispersed throughout the squadron to the appropriate stations and as per other ships' demands and needs," Casper ordered. People around started to whisper, no one liked to be robbed of their ship nor their crew's identity. Tara didn't look any more impressed then anyone else.

"Commander Tyson isn't going to take this lying down, sir," she hissed.

"She already has." Casper smiled sarcastically. "Now I suggest you go start divvying up your crew."

"Sir, this is ridiculous, the *Spartan* is..."

"NOTHING!! Lieutenant, I will have your command if you do not get the fuck out of my sight now and start disbanding your former crew!!" Casper growled. The dizziness returned, Casper's stomach churned slightly with queasiness. He dropped his head again and sucked in a deeper breath than before, closing his eyes.

"Captain Hawk, are you alright?" someone asked.

"Fine," Casper waved them off. However, he didn't look up for fear that the dizziness would get worse. "You're all dismissed, go back to your ships and prepare to accept the *Spartan*'s crew." There was a pause but the shuffle of feet told him the room was emptying. When he finally worked up the courage to open his eyes, he was alone in the large cargo bay.

Where was Harper with that hypo-spray? Casper started toward the door, but his legs were giving way. He bumped into a few chairs before clutching a table and then stooped to his knees.

"Not good," Casper breathed. "Oh boy, not good." Now he was on his hands and knees and blood dripped from his nose. "Calm down, Casper, calm down...that's it...calm down." This wasn't working, Casper slowly sank to the floor his head spinning, he needed help.

"Casper? You still in here?" Harper's voice sounded like a choir of angels.

"Sean!" Casper squeaked from the floor. Harper came into view and his eyes went huge.

"Oh shit, Cass, I leave you alone for two seconds..." Harper sighed. “Come on, let’s get you to the infirmary.” Casper shook his head.

“The crew can’t see me this pathetic,” he said.

“Fine, to your quarters, and I’ll call the doctor from there,” Harper said. He put Casper’s arm over his shoulder and helped the weakened man to his feet. “Man, have you gained weight?”

“Shut up, smart ass,” Casper snarled. Harper laughed and they left the cargo bay.

CHAPTER SEVEN

Later, Casper was lying in his bed feeling slightly better and going over some star charts. They had gotten on their way through the rip, two by two ships were traveling through. Casper was now on the other side of the rip, holding position waiting for the last of the ships to come through. Turns out they had crossed an entire region of space and were dangerously close to the bad border of the Achilles quadrant.

The crew of the *Spartan* was holed up in the cargo bay as slowly they were shuttled to the other ships. The *Spartan* itself had been landed on the surface of Luna Three with a communique to Hearth to come get it and tow it back. Harper had visited the *Spartan*'s crew and returned to Casper telling him that they were all looking like death warmed over.

It was understandable; they put their heart and souls into that ship only to have it taken away from them. He was also made aware that Isis and Danielle were out for his head. Fortunately, the doctor had said he was off limits to everyone including those two. Now he examined how they were going to proceed now that they were finally settled in their voyage.

Beep, beep. Casper looked up to his door and sighed then looked back to his charts. Harper knew he could just come in and anyone else wasn't supposed to be there. *Beep, beep.* The person clearly hadn't gotten the memo that he was supposed to be left alone. *Beep, beep. Beep, beep. Beep, beep. Beep, beep.*

"Holy hell come in already!!!" Casper strained. It hurt his lungs to scream like that, but the person was relentlessly, physically and mentally, pushing his buttons.

She flew in the room like a tornado on steroids, never did Casper think it was possible to contain all the furies of hell into one human body. Her hand came up and down before he could even react to thinking about stopping it and smacked him hard across the face. He didn't reply, he didn't have the energy, he knew this was coming and knew he'd have to face the music. He had had time to think about his comments and actions toward Lt. Pratt and involving the *Spartan*'s situation. While he didn't think about what he decided to do with the crew and ship of the *Spartan*, he knew he could have handled it better, chosen his words better.

As wildly and as harshly as he had been assaulted, the same individual kissed him with as much enthusiasm as the hand had come down.

"What the hell?" he exclaimed as she pulled away.

"Damn it, Casper, how could you be so insensitive? How could you make that comment in front of the entire Squadron? When I wasn't there to…" Danielle stopped short and clutched her side. Clearly she was still hurting and shouldn't be tramping about like an elephant.

"Dani, sit down please," Casper said gently. Danielle did so and leaned on the wall beside him. "I'm sorry for what I said, but tell me you didn't…you know…for that night because you didn't want me to find out about your ship." Danielle turned her upper body toward him and looked him straight in the eye.

"Casper, I don't know what you think goes through my head, but if you really think I would do that to you…well then I guess you've already made your choice," Danielle said. She stood up slowly, her face creased with pain as she did.

"Dani, I'm sorry," Casper said. "I got carried away…I…Sitting in that meeting today it finally sunk in that I don't have much time left." Casper looked to his hands that were pale like the rest of his skin and opened them, palms up. "I'm dying and…and it scares the crap out of me. I don't want to die, young, alone, and on a mission that's almost as pointless as me trying to pretend I'm okay." When Casper looked up Danielle's eyes had gone soft, as had her warrior-like stance. She shook her head and climbed back onto the bed beside him and pulled him into her arms.

"You aren't alone, and the doctors back on Hearth are trying to make an antidote. All hope isn't lost, Casper," Danielle replied.

"I wish I could believe that," he whispered.

"I told you, stop living for the future, live in the moment," Danielle replied. She pressed her lips against his neck and then to his lips. She pulled away and lay next to him and laughed. "If I weren't hurting so bad right now…"

"I don't think either of us have the energy *mi amore*, I think maybe just sitting here would be nice," Casper smiled.

"Mmm…it would, *if* we were together," Danielle said. She stood up off the bed and smiled gently. "That night we spent together wasn't about my ship, it was about the knuckle sandwich I gave you when we were teens, it was about all those times I watched you do your thing in the field of battle and forced myself to concentrate…I *made* love to you that night because I was *in* love with you that night and I still am. But like I said, Isis and I have an understanding with each other. We both have feelings for you, Casper, you need to make a choice."

"A choice," Casper snorted, he looked up to the ceiling. "You know I'll make that a priority over finding Atkinson, and…oh that's right, dying." Danielle laughed and shook her head.

"You aren't dead yet and maybe the doctors will find something," she said. "If and when they do you can't be with both of us, you'll end up…"

"Losing both, I know," Casper sighed. "I know I've got to make up my mind. I'm working on it…that and…" Casper stopped as a radiating pain rode up his left side. "Ah son of a bitch!" he exclaimed. Danielle was instantly at his side.

"Casper what is it? What's wrong?"

"Pain…searing…pain," Casper gasped. He could feel the blood start to trickle down his face again as the pain increased. "God…I'm not ready to die yet," Casper wailed. The pain subsided on his side only to focus itself in his brain and with everything going on up there Casper relented and gave into the overwhelming pull into oblivion. He passed out just before hearing Danielle's worried cry into the com panel for help.

A lot of people had shown up to see the graduating class receive their plaques and command pins. The regular graduates had received their certificates already and stood behind the select command few that Casper was a part of now. Individuals who had shown superior leadership, communication and tactical skills that had been chosen by their instructors and approved by the counsel.

Casper had been to these graduation ceremonies before but had never seen this many people show up. He knew somehow it was because of him and his success as second prince of Hearth in the military. That fact had been run into him many times during basic, and he was finally managing to balance out the prince and the soldier.

Many times during basic had other students made fun of him or showed him very little respect because he was in fact a prince. Several probably still thought the only reason he was in this row of select few was because of his "connections" and who his father was. Casper's instructors had said otherwise, they knew he was there because of his father, but that only made him better and easier to train. He had found out only moments ago that many of his instructors saw him as a natural-born leader like his father and that Casper had earned his place at the top of the command group. One day the squadron would be his to command, his instructors had told him so and knew he was the right man for the job.

So now he stood starchy uniform and pristine boots, hair cropped short under the dress uniforms proud looking cover. Out of the corner of his eye he could see Danielle, also perfectly at ease waiting further command. In spite of their first meeting almost two years ago that ended with Casper sporting a black eye for several weeks, Danielle had turned out to be a formidable ally and even maybe, just maybe a friend.

Casper had been top of his class, yet there was one area no one could touch Danielle's record. That was reaction time. They all knew the "torture" chamber all too well. It was a chamber no bigger than a bedroom that produced images of the enemy in any area. The images would come out and attack so fast that a soldier barely had time to pull out a weapon of any kind or even stop the attacker before they were thrown to the ground mercilessly. Many a soldier had broken, strained, pulled, or torn something in that image chamber, which was why it was nicknamed the "torture" chamber. One other reason was it was all in zero gravity, so the enemy could pin you from the ceiling and you'd have no idea. Casper himself was still nursing a sprained wrist from the last time he had to face that thing.

Danielle, however, was a story all her own in that chamber. She seemed to have a sixth sense, almost know when and where the bad guy was coming from. Many times Casper and several other recruits would watch her in the chamber as she bounced off walls with lightening quickness leaving the enemy hologram in one last frozen pose before she blew their head off. Some people said she was part Liomenin wild cat.

Liomenin was a one of the many planets traveled to and explored by humans, the wild cats that lived there looked like any normal large cat found on Hearth or even the old Earth save for one exception. The Liomenin cat, if necessary, could go one hundred and twenty miles per hour, one second it was in front of you, the next it was half way across the plains. To date, no human had ever caught a Liomenin cat or even caught a good picture of one.

That was Danielle, that was how fast she could think, how fast she could move; it was an awesome sight to behold. Harper would always joke that if they ever needed someone to go into a dangerous situation, she would be it because if required she could get out before anyone knew she had gone in.

Which brought Casper's thoughts to Harper. He had always

thought it would be cool if Harper could be a captain of a ship along with him but unfortunately his friend just barely missed the cut. When they found out who had made what position Casper could see the slight disappointment in his friend's eyes and tried to encourage his friend that all was not lost. After all Harper was in the group of soldiers standing directly behind Casper and that was the line of seconds. Should any of Casper's line fail to maintain expectations or higher expectations they'd be removed from training or moved back in training and one of the seconds would move up.

Casper tried to peer around to see Harper but his position wouldn't allow it, so he settled for the fact of knowing his friend was right there. The two had also made a promise that no matter what, they'd always stick together like a team. Casper would never let Harper be anywhere but at his side as second in command of whatever ship he may be on.

Around the parade square behind the counsel Casper could see his mom and dad and Maverick sitting and watching. Casper's dad had a huge smile on his face as he sat almost bursting at the seems with pride, and his mother, ever the diplomatic one, sat just as proud pointing out to anyone that was in earshot that the boy in the center was her son and he had earned it on his own.

Casper himself was filled with pride at making his parents so proud of him, but at the same time he still couldn't help but feel slightly jealous that it was Maverick who sat beside them and not him. Maverick had been going through all kinds of political schooling and debating classes and they had paid off, his brother was Hearth champion in almost every debate he had ever been in.

Ah the aid of being a prince. Casper hated it, he didn't want to be known as a prince, he wanted to be known as the soldier he was now and forever will be. Hopefully things would change as he went on to battle the fundamentalists. The thought was that the farther he got from Hearth the less and less his prince title would hold any value.

"Ladies and gentlemen of the court, guests and our sovereign leaders, it is my pleasure to give you this year's graduating class. They have worked hard and no doubt will be a great value to us in the future," announced the current commander of ground forces. Then the man turned to the class, ordered them to attention and dismissed them to their families and friends.

Casper and Harper found each other instantly and gave each other high fives.

"We kick ass!!!!" Harper exclaimed. "You're the *man,* Cass!!"

"No *you* are!!!" Casper laughed back.

"Man, we are going to be an awesome team. We are going to bring the wars to an end because of how good we are!" Harper said.

"If Danielle doesn't get there first!" Casper joked. Harper made a face and rolled his eyes.

"Her? She's harmless, yeah she can move fast but...Oooow!!!" Danielle has snuck up behind Harper and pinched him on the arm. Casper saw she really got a good chunk on his arm too and laughed.

"You were saying?" she asked innocently. Harper was rubbing his arm with a sore look on his face.

"Ow," he replied. Danielle laughed and patted him on the shoulder and then turned to Casper and extended her hand.

"Congrats, Casper, you deserve it."

"I do?" Casper eyed her hand wearily, all through basic she had been a friend but never really admitted when someone had done better than her or let alone deserve something over her.

"Yes, I'm glad my parents made me wait a year to train with you. I've learned a lot from your style and way of thinking, you could even say I'm almost...*impressed,*" Danielle said. Casper's eyes went huge as he shook her hand as did Harper's who leaned in over the handshake and looked at her.

"Did *you* just say you were *impressed* by what someone *else* did?" he asked.

"Don't get used to it, boys, it was a one-time thing," she replied. "None the less..." Danielle gave Casper a quick peck on the cheek before locating her parents and running off into her father's proud outstretched arms. Casper stood dumbfounded at what had just happened, then slowly he turned to Harper just as shocked. Gradually both of them started smiling and nodded.

"ALRIGHT!!!" they both said in unison and gave each other another high five.

"Oh there's my dad!" Harper exclaimed. Casper watched his friend take off toward his father and decided it would be good to go in search of his own parents. He walked around the crowds of people but couldn't find them. It actually came to a point were he wondered if they had left already, maybe Maverick had a debate or some stupid class to get to and heaven forbid they should miss that.

Just when Casper was about to call it quits and find a royal guard to get a ride back to the palace someone ripped his cover off his head and ruffled his hair with a laugh.

"MAV! Give it back!!" Casper whined. His family appeared out of the crowd and his mother gave him a huge hug then let his father do the same. "Where have you guys been?" Casper asked, slightly hurt that it had taken them that long to get to him.

"Damn it all if everyone wants to congratulate us on our son's job well done." Anthony smiled. "We tried really, but there are so many people here."

"I get it," Casper said still slightly unimpressed.

"We are SO proud of you, Casper, your father's been bursting at the seems for this day and he hasn't been able to stop smiling!" Patricia smiled. Casper looked at his father who still wore the smile of a proud father, somehow his parents' happiness made him forget the slight feeling of abandonment he had felt earlier and smiled back.

"I have to admit, Cass, you look good in that uniform." Maverick shrugged.

"Good god," Casper joked. "Another compliment from someone least likely to give it!" He filled them in on the conversation with Danielle and even the slight peck on the cheek.

"Ooooo, someone's got a crush on you!" Maverick joked. Casper punched him in the arm and took back his cover and placed it back on his head.

"I've been waiting years to be able to do this to one of you..." Anthony smiled. With that he snapped to attention in his own uniform and performed a crisp salute, soldier to superior. Casper mimicked the move and saluted back with just as much professionalism. After which both broke out into laughter and Anthony pulled his son into a headlock hug.

"Come now! We have to get back to the palace and get ready for the dinner for the command graduates!" Patricia said. It was a custom that a dinner be held the night of graduation for the command graduates, they and their families would come to the palace and there would be a feast. However something about this irked Casper.

"Mom?" he asked.

"What is it, Casper?"

"Can we make this a special case and bring the entire grad class? I have friends and well…" Casper trailed off realizing his request was no small task.

"Done, we can extend the celebrations from the ballroom to the main hall, we can fit everyone," Patricia smiled. Casper smiled broadly and pumped his fist in glee.

"Sweeeet!" he exclaimed. "Give me two seconds, I have to tell my friends!" Casper ran off to find Harper and break the good news. Somehow his friends and future crew's opinion meant more to him than anything in the world. He saw Harper and Danielle along with one or two other friends of his and started waving his arms. "Hey guys!! Guess what???" Their smiles all grew with the news and Casper received many pats on the back.

Thwack! Crash! Thud! Casper opened on eye and looked at the rug under his head and up to the edge of the bed he just rolled off and then back down to the shattered picture frame by his hand that had suffered the wrath of his attempt to stay in bed. Oddly enough, his hand that had borne the brunt of the night table and picture frame, wasn't bleeding much and barely hurt.

Casper looked at his hand and brought it to his face, then retracted it quickly—ice! It felt as cold as ice! He checked again just to make sure it was in fact his hand and sure enough, his hand was nearly frozen.

Shaking it off, Casper clutched the bed and had much difficulty getting himself to his feet. It was almost as if his entire body had cramped up, but being the stubborn man he was he did his best to leave his room and head to the bridge. He was just about to round the main corner to the bridge when he heard his name being mentioned, so he stopped and listened. It instantly became clear that it was a discussion about him involving three people who meant the most to him, Danielle, Isis, and Harper. It gave him all the more reason to listen to what they were really thinking about him.

"So what did the doctor say?"

"At the rate he's going, the way he's pushing himself, doc says he's shortening his weeks to days."

"It's not fair, none of this is *fair*."

"Tell me about it…what are we supposed to do? He's got to slow down, I've been in touch with Hearth and the doctors say they've made a promising start but nothing solid yet. We have *got* to get him to slow down."

"Sean, don't you think we know that? Hell we're the women who are in love with him."

"Yeah…that's kind of weird how you two are getting along as well as you are."

"He's *dying,* you insensitive prick! If we can ease his mind by still being in love with him and not cat fighting about trying to sway him either way then that's what we'll do."

"Don't you ever say that again!" Harper's voice got slightly high pitch when he spoke. "He's *not* dying, he *can't* die, he's…he's my friend! He's not going to die, I won't let him!" There was a pause in the conversation and then a soft female voice.

"It may not be up to you, Sean, you can't always protect him like you did in basic," Danielle soothed. Casper's brow furrowed in curiosity and disapproval.

"I did what I had to in basic, you shouldn't bring that up so many years later. He was the Prince of Hearth, you really think I'm going to let him not make it through the first week? Besides in the end it was all him."

"He would have made it through without that."

"No, he wouldn't have, if I didn't change those com, nav directions he inputted into his test ship on the fourth day of training his team would have gotten lost in space. By the time the instructors would have found him, he would have jumped to deep space and enemy territory! They would have all been killed, Dani!" Casper was shocked, horrified was a better word, and he sank to the floor and ran his hands through his long hair, pulling out the tie that bound it. His long black hair fell shedding down beside his face as he tried to control his emotions. All those people who said he was there because he was a prince, all the effort he had put forth to ridding himself of that title, everything he did to get where he was…he didn't deserve any of it, he was supposed to be dead!

"They would have got to him in time…but that's in the past; he's a kick-ass leader now and that's the man we all care about. How are we supposed to tell him, Danielle, that we want him to step back and let us handle this?"

"I don't know, Harper."

"We've got to do it somehow and we've got to do it soon, by any means necessary."

"I don't think I like where this is going, Crewmen Soul, not at all."

"No, Dani, I think she's right, I think any means necessary is what it's going to take."

"You two are insane! Are you really considering mutiny? Against the Centaury Zebra Squadron leader and the second prince to the throne of Hearth Condes, are you???" Casper lifted his head slightly curious to hear the answer.

"It's to save his life, Lieutenant, to keep him alive long enough to at least see Atkinson captured…"

"Captured? I'm blowing the monster's head into every corner of the universe when I find him, and then I'm going to burn his ashes, piss on them, and do a little dance!! That…that substandard, vile, worm of a human being tortured both Maverick and I and forced us to watch while they…took away his livelihood! You weren't there! You didn't hear him scream! Blood freezing, ear splitting, torturous screams!"

"Sean-Patrick…I thought Maverick was the only one who…"

"So does he and so does Casper and that's the way it's going to stay, neither of them were conscious enough to know I was in the room. Atkinson's minions didn't find me interesting enough to beat me into confusion, so they just made me watch…I wasn't high up enough on the food chain for them to give a damn, okay? So help me if you tell anyone about this." Casper was floored, Harper had seen just as much as Maverick had, enough not more, but it didn't make sense. Why wouldn't Harper tell him? Weren't they supposed to be friends?

"This is out of hand."

"I know, but I think we should talk to him; nonetheless, he needs to stop trying so hard and start thinking about himself."

"Okay, okay, so who's going to do it?" Again another pause, this time fire burned Casper's insides. He suddenly felt a rage and betrayal that he had never felt before. His best friend lied to him; the two women he was in love with lied to him. He felt like he was all alone with no one to count on, in his last dying days he suddenly was completely, utterly deserted…and he hated everyone for it…all of them.

Suppressing his tears and anger as best as possible Casper stood back up and took a deep breath.

"Why don't one of you do it?"

"Because, Harper, we aren't his best friend since he was a baby."

"So you come up with the idea but pin it on me?? How is that fair."

"You said it yourself, none of this is fair." That was the last straw. Casper, as stiff as his frozen limbs were, stood tall and rounded the corner. All three of them froze, mortified in their tracks and stared at him. He said nothing, nothing at all, he just looked each one of them in the eye. Casper wanted them to see the anger, betrayal, pain, emptiness, and loss that he felt. He wanted them to feel as bad as he did at the moment, and it was clear by the looks on their faces that he was succeeding and then some.

"How much did you hear?" Harper asked quietly. Casper didn't say anything, he was still much, much too angry to say anything.

"Casper?" Danielle asked.

"We didn't mean to hurt you," Isis added. Casper finally looked past them and started walking right by them without even a word. He didn't look at them as he walked by, he looked straight ahead and kept on walking.

Back on the bridge Casper took a deep breath and sat in his chair.

"What's our status Ensign Maddox?" he asked.

"Commander Tyson ordered the fleet into enemy territory, there was some evidence of activity near one of the furthermost moons of Denora. Is there a change of plans, sir?" Freddy asked.

"No, no change, tell me when did you think it okay to take orders from Commander Tyson?" Casper growled. Freddy turned around looking very, very confused.

"Uh…sir?" he asked.

"Were you or were you not aware the command staff of the *Spartan* was relieved of duty?" he asked.

"Yes, sir but I figured…"

"Figure nothing, you followed someone who's got even less pull than you do Maddox, but I'm letting it go this time," Casper replied.

"Sir, Lt. Harper said that it would be okay, Captain," Linda said from the communication console. Casper looked over at her and clenched his jaw.

"Lt. Harper said, hmm? Tell me Ensign Park, you *supposedly* went through the academy, what's rule number five of the military charter?" he asked. Linda thought for a second and then spoke.

"If one's captain is unable to perform his or her duties, the second in command of his or her vessel is to take charge, maintain a neutral circumstance until the captain is able to say otherwise or the captain returns to full duty," Linda replied. "Direct quote, chapter two of the academy text, page 24, any more questions?"

"Don't get smart," Casper hissed. "In any case, Ensign Maddox should you have been told to do anything else than what is in the book you should have disobeyed until *I* told you otherwise."

"Sorry, Captain," Freddy replied. Casper shook his head, he was getting mad at the wrong people.

"No, I'm sorry, to the both of you," he said and looked over at Linda who smiled back.

"Now, how long until we get to the planned coordinates?" Casper asked. Freddy turned back to his console and pressed a few buttons.

"Approximately a day more travel, sir," he replied. Casper sighed.

"At top speed?" he asked.

"Well not for us but some of the older ships haven't had our upgrades so they can't move as fast; we outrun them and we lose several of the fleet," Freddy answered. Casper took a deep breath and slowly nodded then turned toward the lift.

"Did Lt. Harper say when he'd be back?" Casper asked.

"He and the commander just stepped out with one of the engineers," Linda replied.

"Leaving *who* exactly in charge of a twenty-two ship squadron in enemy territory?" Casper asked. Freddy looked over at Linda and then to the two other soldiers at panels at the back of the bridge, then back to Casper and shrugged.

"I guess Ensign Park has seniority in the room right now," he resolved. Casper turned to Linda who looked as surprised as the others in the room.

"Did you know you were in charge, Ensign? Did you know if the squadron were to come under attack at this moment it would be *you* who would be responsible for giving directions? Or did *someone* neglect to inform you of that?" he asked. Linda looked dumbfounded and shocked.

"Well, I guess I didn't technically know it was me, but I guess if something had happened I would have assumed command," she replied.

"Fucking wonderful, well you have the bridge, Ensign, I'll be in the mess hall if you need me." Casper sighed. Linda nodded and moved over to the captain's chair where she should have been when Casper walked in. He shook his head and walked off the bridge toward the lift.

Moments later Casper walked into the mess hall and headed to the captain's mess. Inside the cook took his order and Casper sat back thinking.

"What a life huh, Cass?" he asked himself. Once again he untied the leather strap holding back his hair and let it fall loose again. He ran his hands through it a few times and then slouched back in his chair and looked out at the stars whizzing past. They were so simplistic billions of miles away, floating balls of rock or gas.

Beep, beep.

"Come in." Thinking it was chef with his food Casper casually called the person in. His food did come in, however, it was not being carried by the chef but rather by Isis.

"This I don't need," Casper sighed.

"Hear me out please?" Isis asked. She set his food down in front of him and stood behind the chair across from Casper.

"You have five minutes," he said. "You might as well sit." He started into his food as she spoke, not so much because he was hungry but rather in a way to avoid making eye contact with her.

"I've decided something, Casper, you may not like it but I've come to a decision," Isis said.

"Oh yeah? And what's that?" he asked between bites.

"You and Danielle are meant to be. I'm making your life slightly easier by making that one choice for you," Isis replied. Casper had no choice but to look up at her to see if she was serious. Her face was dead serious.

"So, I'm dying faster than expected and you think by saying you don't want to be with me anymore it's going to make everything alright?" Casper asked. Isis shook her head and fiddled with the sleeve of her uniform.

"No, but seeing Commander Tyson crumple in a heap of body-wracking, inconsolable sobs I realized that as deep as I feel for you, she loves you just that much more. Right now Harper is still trying to get her to stop crying, telling her that it's okay, she hasn't lost you. I feel horrible for what you must have heard as well, but you need to talk to her," Isis said. Casper laughed sarcastically and shook his head.

"Yes, because *that's* the biggest issue I have right now with what I heard." Casper sighed. "You three…you were planning a mutiny, you were planning on…whatever, I don't care about what you were planning to do, it's the fact that you three, my closest allies turned on me in the blink of an eye. The fact that Harper has been lying to me for so long I…I don't know whom I'm supposed to trust now." Isis reached across the table and took Casper's hand in hers. He was surprised she didn't react to the frigidness of his hands but rather held them tightly trying to warm.

"Trust me, here and now, I'm telling you the three of us were thinking of nothing but you when we started that conversation. You can't block us out of your life, not now, not when you need us the most. Think of Danielle if nothing else, she loves you with every fiber of her being and can barely function now because of it," she said gently. Casper looked into her eyes and saw nothing but innocence and truth. He sighed heavily and nodded.

"I can't believe you're doing this, trying so hard to get me to take another woman into my arms," he said.

"I just know how to choose my battles, sweetheart." She smiled.

"You're an angel, Isis, have I ever told you that? I hope this doesn't ruin the bond we've formed. I mean…you really are special to me," Casper smiled.

"I know, hon, but I'm not the woman you're meant to be with." Isis smiled. "You need to talk to her and Harper." At that Casper pulled his hand away and sighed looking away from Isis.

"Danielle yes, Harper…I don't think so," he replied. "I've been with that man since birth and he's a total stranger; I don't like strangers."

"Well, I think you should, but…I won't push you, just know I'm here for you, as a friend that is." Isis smiled. She leaned over and gave Casper a peck on the cheek before getting up and disappearing out the door. Casper looked at the plateful of food in front of him, suddenly he wasn't hungry. It was probably all for the best as he had exactly a day to make sure all affairs were in order, including Danielle. Pushing the food aside Casper got up and went off in search of Danielle.

He found her in the leisure deck. It was empty save her in the corner, staring out a large window at the stars, similar to what he had been doing moments earlier in the captain's mess. From across the room Casper could see the tears fresh on her cheek; she held a Kleenex in hand and sat curled up on the high-ended couch.

"Dani?" Casper said quietly. She turned slowly but when she saw who it was she stood up immediately to face him head on.

"Casper, I…I'm so sorry, please, please forgive me." It was all she managed to get out before bursting into tears again and nearly crumpling to the ground. Isis hadn't been kidding when she said Danielle was breaking apart. Casper got to her side and pulled her into him so she could use him as support. "I'm so sorry," she wailed.

"Shhhh, it's okay, I forgive you, stop crying it's alright," Casper soothed. He guided her back down to the couch and handed her another tissue. She took it gratefully and cleaned up her face then looked at him.

"But you were so angry earlier…" she sniffed.

"I was, but I had some sense talked into me, by Isis actually," Casper replied. Danielle looked almost upset by the news and nodded.

"Oh, so you and she…"

"Are friends, Danielle, I love you," Casper said. Danielle looked like she didn't know what to do with the news. She looked at her hands and then back up to Casper, a smile crept across her face.

"R…really? You mean you and I…?" she sniffed. Casper answered her question by pulling her close to him and kissing her. He pulled away just slightly and leaned his forehead on hers so as to keep the moment of intimacy.

"Dani, no matter what happens, you're in my heart, you have been since basic when you gave me that peck on the cheek at graduation of basic. I don't want you to suffer if I die, you need to be ready to accept it," he whispered. Danielle nodded, the tears still fresh on her face.

"I know, I know, but the doctors are working for a cure, maybe they'll find something, maybe…"

"Aren't you the one always telling me to live in the moment?"

Casper smiled gently. Danielle let out a short laugh and hugged Casper tightly.

"Oh Casper, I love you too, and yes...let's live in the moment." She smiled.

"Your quarters or mine?" Casper said wiggling his eyebrows. Danielle adjusted her position so as to be much, *much* closer to him and went to whisper in his ear.

"I ordered everyone out of the leisure deck, told them to give me two hours...I've still got an hour and twenty minutes," she said. Casper had to laugh.

"You wicked, evil woman." She moved swiftly and straddled Casper's lap and wrapped her arms around his neck.

"You know it," she smiled mischievously, "and now that you're mine, things could get *very* interesting." Casper laughed but was cut short when Danielle hungrily moved in for a deep kiss.

Casper had a bit more of a bounce in his step later that day. He and Danielle decided for the morale of her own ship's crew it would be good for her to shuttle between all the ships to speak with them. Isis however had decided to stay in the Specter's engineering room, feeling it best if she were on the ship in case Casper needed a friend. The only black cloud however that hung over him was the one issue he had fortunately managed to avoid thus far, Harper. The man had simply managed to make himself scarce, probably a good idea, considering Casper just wasn't sure what he would say should he come across the man.

Casper sat in his chair with just a few hours to go when he realized he still hadn't seen hide nor hair of Harper since that morning. His feeling of anger was starting to subside into worry. If Harper had been forced to watch everything Maverick had and more maybe he was actually hurting much more then he let on.

He pushed the com button on his own console and spoke. "Hawk to Lt. Harper..." Then he waited. After no response he tried again, "Captain Hawk to Lt. Harper, come in lieutenant." After a second paused he looked to Linda who had an expression of uncertainty about her. In his own seat, Freddy had flat out turned to look at Casper not being discreet at all. Casper turned to one of the crewmen behind him, "Locate Lt. Harper," he ordered.

"He's in his quarters, sir," the crewman replied seconds later. Casper was already on his feet.

"Linda, you have the bridge," he said half way off the bridge.

As Casper made his way to Harper's room he seemed to have the increased feeling deep in his gut that something wasn't right. Harper wouldn't just not respond even knowing Casper was upset with him, he knew to keep professional and friendships separate. Casper started into a light jog to get to his friend's room. One or two soldiers looked at him as he jogged past no doubt wondering what the rush was but he ignored them, as he ignored the strain the light jog was putting on his lungs.

He reached Harper's room and pressed the call button, once, twice, and again but received no answer. Now Casper was worried, all anger aside he was worried that his friend was going to do something stupid or worse still *had* done something stupid. Finally Casper decided to override the door lock and entered Harper's room.

"Sean-Patrick?" he asked the silence. A slight noise caught his attention from the sitting room of the quarters. He went over there cautiously not wanting to startle his friend. As he stuck his head into the room he saw Harper immediately, the room's lights were dimmed low or off, Casper couldn't quite tell. Harper sat in a chair just in the shadows of the window where some light might be shed from passing stars.

"Harper, what's going on? Why didn't you answer those calls?" Casper asked.

"Guess I wasn't paying attention." Harper's voice was low and weak, something was wrong, very wrong. Casper started to squint, he was trying to see more than just Harper's legs and the dark shadow he sat in.

"Are you okay?" Casper asked. There was a pause, a strange long drawn-out pause that made Casper very nervous.

"You shouldn't be here," Harper said finally.

"Does that mean you aren't okay?" Casper replied almost immediately. Again another eerie pause.

"You shouldn't be here," Harper said again.

"Screw if I should be here or not, Sean, tell me what's wrong," Casper replied.

"I can't," Harper answered. His voice was almost a whisper now, it didn't sound like him at all.

"Tell me what's wrong and maybe I can help," Casper urged. He was barely aware of what he was saying, he just wanted to get Harper out of the dark shadow.

"You should go now," Harper replied. Casper ignored the statement completely.

"Can I turn on the light, Sean?"

"No."

"Will you come out of the corner then?"

"No." Casper sighed, whatever was wrong Harper didn't seem to want any company dealing with it. Still Casper was very reluctant to leave his friend when the man didn't seem himself at all.

"Sean, I'm sorry I didn't say anything when I overheard your conversation earlier. I was just…angry I guess, that I had been lied to," Casper said. He was hoping by bringing up the reason this was probably happening, Harper would be provoked into saying more about what exactly the problem was.

"Apology accepted," Harper said stoically. Casper took a step forward but stopped when he saw his friend flinch.

"Talk to me, Sean, please," he asked.

"No."

"Why not?"

"I can't." This time Harper's quiet whispered voice sounded like he may have started to cry. Finally Casper sighed, they were talking in circles, it was clear that Harper wanted to be alone at the moment so Casper backed toward the door.

"Okay, Harp, I'm leaving but promise me you'll talk to me when you're ready. We really need to talk, you and I, but I'm not upset anymore, just worried about you, much as I am my own brother." He sighed. Then he turned and walked out of the room. He paused for a second in the bedroom wondering if he was doing the right thing and then continued to the door.

"Cass?" Casper whirled around when the weak voice appeared to be in the door way behind him. Casper was horrified, Harper leaned almost all his weight on the doorway. His face was stained with tears but worst of all there was a sheen of red blood trailing down both arms. The blood was still flowing, gushing rather from two identical wounds on either of his wrists.

"Oh sweet Jesus," Casper gasped. He started toward Harper and caught him just in time before he collapsed to the floor.

"You shouldn't be here," Harper cried. "You weren't supposed to be here." As quickly as his own stiff body would allow Casper ripped the sheets from the bed and wrapped them tightly around his friend's wrists. Then he raced to the com panel and called for a medical emergency in Harper's room before getting back to his friend's side. Harper was now barely conscious.

"Why, Harp, why would you do this?" Casper asked.

"They wouldn't let me turn away, they held me face forward and kept me awake," Harper cried. "Every moment, every horrible moment, and they laughed at me, there was nothing I could do but watch. They told me it was my fault, if I closed my eyes or turned my head they said that was making it worse for you…It was my fault, we got abducted because of me and there was nothing I could do…nothing." Casper's heart sank, his friend was blaming himself for those weeks of hell they had been put through. Worse still it appeared that Harper had been mentally abused to a severe degree.

"Harper, you did nothing wrong!" Casper replied.

"I did, you know it, you looked at me and I saw it in your eyes, then and today…I lied to you and I couldn't keep you safe like I promised your parents…I, I'm so…sorry," Harper choked. When Harper's eyes started to flutter shut Casper started to shake him gently.

"Harper, come on now don't close your eyes," Casper urged. But it wasn't enough as soon Harper's head slumped to one side, unconscious. “Harperrrrrrrrrrrrrrr…” Casper groaned. Just then the medical staff came running in the door.

“What happened?” the doctor asked incredulously.

“I should have seen it coming, I was too busy worrying about my own problems.” Casper shook his head. The doctor put a hand on his shoulder as Harper was carried off to sickbay.

“Never blame yourself, no one ever sees this coming,” she soothed. “Captain, I need you to come to infirmary with me, the doctors on Hearth Condes think they’re on to something, but they need more blood from you.”

“Great, just what I need,” Casper sighed. Then he nodded, “I was going there anyway.”

Upon arriving at the infirmary Casper immediately contacted the bridge and told Linda to stop the fleet because of an emergency. Casper had felt the ship stop when they were taking his blood and was almost relieved that he didn’t have to fight any battles just yet.

“Okay, Captain, the samples have been sent, you can go if you want.” The doctor smiled. Casper didn’t even consider the thought for a second.

“How is the lieutenant?” he asked. The doctor frowned, never a good sign and spoke.

“He’s lost a lot of blood, it’s a miracle you found him when you did because any longer and…well it’s a good thing you found him,” she replied. “He’s recovering physically, with much more rest and some infusions he’ll be back to normal.”

“What about operational?” Casper asked. The doctor shook her head without hesitation.

“Not for a while, he needs counseling and lots of it; what he *needs* is to be brought back to Hearth Condes,” she replied. Casper sighed and ran his hand down his face in exhaustion. “Due respect, sir, you could do nicely with the atmosphere of home.”

“Not now, not after we’ve come this far,” Casper replied. He sat back down on the nearby med bed and sighed, he was so tired.

“Let’s say you get Atkinson, what good will it be if you can’t bring him back to Hearth for trial? I looked at your blood myself and the erosion that's happened since this journey started is ten-fold what was expected," she said.

"What are you saying, doctor?" Casper asked, afraid to find out the answer.

"I'm saying…as hard as it is for someone who's been with your family for so long, I believe that due to the cellular degeneration rate it's a wonder you're still standing," she said quietly. This time Casper had to lower his head between his legs to breath deeply.

"Oh god," he breathed.

"There was no way to know the pathogen would be so aggressive," the doctor said. Casper didn't know what to think or say, his months had become days, which had become mere hours. Suddenly Harper came into his head, after all the man had done for Casper he was letting him down by dying too soon. Harper had done nothing but protect him and worship everything he did and always gave him the confidence he needed to keep going. Harper was his second brother, lying in the other room fighting for his life.

"I want to see the lieutenant," Casper said quietly.

"Certainly, this way," she motioned. Casper followed her to the other room of sickbay, the closed private room that Danielle had been in earlier. At the door the doctor stopped and held out her hand to Casper. "Be aware that he's very, very unstable right now, he's been through an ordeal, as you were a witness for." Casper nodded and thanked the doctor then headed into the room.

The room carried the somber mood of the occupant inside. Casper's first instinct was to check the bed for Harper but soon found out the bed, though rumpled, was empty. Harper stood staring at a picture on the wall, but Casper couldn't really tell if he was looking at the photo or if he was just using it as something to focus on.

Casper entered the room and sat down, but said nothing because he thought it would be better for Harper to make the first move. The man could be feeling anything at the moment and Casper didn't want to say the wrong thing.

"I'm just worried about you, much as I am my own brother,"

Harper said quietly. His tightly wrapped wrists were curled around his chest hugging himself.

"Pardon?" Casper asked. Harper didn't turn away from the photo.

"You said that to me earlier and that's why I left the corner of the room," Harper explained. "When I was eight and my mother died it was rough on my dad and me. Being the only child I thought I had no one to count on, and then there was your family. Your mom and dad let me and my dad stay in the palace until my dad was ready to go back to work. Even after my dad went back to work your parents said there was no need to move out because the palace was big enough for us to stay. In those years you, Maverick, and I became close and I always wished I was actually your brother. Then you'd go off to your fancy dinners and I was left alone, by myself, to play, alone.

"I convinced myself that maybe, just maybe, if I watched over you as an older brother would, then your family would bring me along to one of your dinners. I love my father I do, but when I saw how happy you and your family was…I was jealous but when ever you could you treated me as one of your own. I owe your family for a happy childhood and my father getting back on his feet…I owe you all that…and I failed. I sat there and watched while everything I worked for got taken away in a matter of days.

"I thought I could get over it, I tried really, but then you found out about basic and then gave me that look. A look that got rid of everything I had ever thought we had bonded together with each other. Sounds stupid, I know, you probably don't think about it nearly as much if at all. I'm sorry I failed you, Casper, and I'm sorry you had to witness what you just did. I hadn't meant for you to see that, but then when you said that line…much as I do my own brother…I knew I was taking the coward's way out, and I knew it wasn't what you'd want." Harper continued to stare at the photo on the wall. Now Casper knew it didn't matter what was in the frame, it was just something to stare at. However, finally Harper looked away from the photo to his wrists.

"*This* is not what you'd want," Harper said quietly. Casper was amazed at how strong Harper had remained throughout his entire life. It hadn't just been since the abduction, it had been since his mother died that this emotion had been building.

"No, it wasn't and it's true Sean-Patrick, I've always thought of you as a brother. Sometimes even more than I do Maverick," Casper replied. Harper finally looked at him, the stain of tears down his face but a look of hope.

"Really?" he asked quietly. Casper nodded and pushed out the chair opposite him for Harper to sit down.

"Maverick is my blood brother, but he didn't go through basic with me, he didn't go through school with me, he hasn't been at my side for the last ten years, and let's face it, you never flipped me onto my stomach to beat me into submission," Casper joked. Harper smiled weakly. "As for me thinking about that as much as you, it's true, I guess I never gave it as much thought as you, but that doesn't mean I didn't wish you were there at every formal dinner I was forced to endure. I hated those things, and I could never wait to rip off that god-awful uniform and go scouting the local university for chicks." Again Harper smiled weakly and even let out a small chuckle.

"Cass, I know you want Atkinson badly but…I…I need to go home. I can take a shuttle if you want but…"

"I'm turning the *Specter* around," Casper's comment caught Harper off guard; he looked almost stunned.

"Why?" he asked. Casper shrugged, tugging on his ponytail and looking at the tips of hair.

"For you, for me, I don't know what changed my mind really, but we should have never left Hearth. I can't say what the other ships are going to do but I want to get home before I…" Casper stopped and lowered his head. "I don't have much time left, Harp, the doctor just told me…I don't want my family to lose the chance to say goodbye." When he looked back up at Harper, his friend was looking at him with a very serious expression.

"I think the other captains will agree with you, a lot of them came up to me before we left and said…damn it, I guess that's something else I kept from you," Harper sighed with a frown.

"Hey, Harp, if you're doing something in my best interest you don't have to tell me if you don't want to or think it'll stress me out. Saying that, you shouldn't ever have to feel you need to go out of your way to protect me, I'm not your responsibility. Man, Harper, you should have come to me sooner, I wish you had," Casper said. "Before it got this bad."

"You know I was planning to actually." Harper sighed.

"When?"

"When your brother and I snuck onto the *Specter* so he could explain himself. I knew this was my opening as well," he responded. Casper sat forward, curious now.

"What stopped you?" he asked.

"We got abducted," Harper said curtly. That was something Casper should have known and felt bad for bringing that up.

"It doesn't matter now, what matters is we get you home so you can get better." Casper smiled.

"And you?" Harper asked quietly. "What's your reason for going home?"

"Atkinson needs to be caught, yes, but look at me, I'm in no condition to lead soldiers into battle and…I've realized how selfish I've been toward everyone, and I know now…I want to die in the warmth of my family," Casper replied. Harper nodded and took a shaky deep breath.

"Dani and Isis aren't going to like this," he said.

"I know, they'll understand."

"They'll get Atkinson though, I know it."

"So do I," Casper replied. "I need to go contact the other captains and inform the crew. The quicker I do, the faster we can get home." Harper nodded but said nothing. Casper could see tears start in his eyes again, so he gave as brave a smile as he could manage and headed out the door.

Just as he exited Isis came up with a look of horror on her face.

"Is it true? Did he really try to…?" she asked. Casper nodded.

"We're going home, Isis, he needs to go home," he said.

"Poor, poor man, do you think he'd mind if I went in?" she asked. Casper thought about it for a second and then smiled.

"He'd probably appreciate it a lot," he replied. Isis gave a nod and headed into the room. Casper didn't walk away right away, he though about Isis being there for Harper and was glad she had come. Sometimes the only thing a man wanted was a woman's touch to calm him.

CHAPTER EIGHT

The other captains didn't even have to think about it, they agreed with Casper but made sure to express that they were honored to serve under him and continue the search for him.

"You said a wise leader knew when he should turn around, Captain, and you've shown us all how much of a great leader you are," Captain Lexis said over the com.

"It's true, Hawk, it's an honor to know you think we can keep going without you," Captain Jeffrey said. "May God give you a safe journey home and speed the doctors' research."

"I thank all of you for following me on this mission and thank you for continuing on under Commander Tyson's command. Truly it has been an honor to serve with you all, and I hope you all have many more years of happy lives with your friends and families. I guess this is goodbye, friends, so for the last time, dismissed and Captain Hawk out." Casper lowered his head and nodded to Linda to close the link. She herself had tears in her eyes, but a smile on her face for his benefit. He smiled at her and then looked to Freddy.

"Ensign, set a course for home, but hold here until I give the go ahead," he ordered.

"Yes, sir." Casper nodded again and headed down to the shuttle bay where the last of the *Spartan*'s crew was getting ready to depart to the *Nautilus*, which Lexis had offered to become the flag ship and also offered to step down so Danielle could assume command.

Down in the shuttle bay Casper and Harper said goodbye to the soldiers and then stepped just outside the door with Isis and Danielle. Both women were fighting tears but not nearly as much as Casper was.

"I…I…just…" Casper didn't know where to begin. Isis went first because she knew he and Danielle would want a private moment.

"You just get home and get better understood?" She smiled. Casper nodded and pulled her into a hug then held her at arms' length.

"Be safe," he said. "And I'd never be where I am today without you." Isis smiled and turned away. Instead of heading back into the shuttle bay she went over to Harper, took his hand, and walked down the hallway so they were out of earshot. Danielle moved to wrap her arms around Casper.

"Wait for me," she said.

"In every sense of the word," Casper replied. They kissed each other deeply and then parted. Oddly enough it was then Casper thought of something totally unrelated to their goodbye. "Danielle, they have a large cloaked ship, set your sensors to radio frequencies and you should be able to create a sonar image on the sensors."

"I'll make sure all the ships know," she said. They paused for a second as Casper realized this might be the last time he ever saw his love.

"Don't you dare go dying before me, you understand? You be careful, in fact, wrap yourself in bubble wrap and tissue paper," Casper said. Danielle let out a laugh between the sobs that had started to overwhelm her.

"My prince," she replied.

"My princess," he added immediately afterward. Once again they kissed as if their lives depended on the intimacy of the kiss and held together until neither of them could hold their breath any longer. "Go," Casper whispered. Without another word Danielle disappeared into the shuttle bay. She knew as well as he that if they held each other any longer they wouldn't be able to separate.

Casper then turned his attention over to Harper and Isis; they gave each other a hug and a kiss. Then Isis headed toward the shuttle door pausing briefly to give Casper one last peck on the cheek goodbye.

Once the shuttle had departed from the ship Casper pressed the com button and called the bridge.

"Take us home, Freddy," he said.

"Aye, sir," came the reply. The ship shuddered slightly as she turned away from the formation and back in the direction of home. Casper took a long, drawn out deep breath and then nodded his head. It was over, they were on their way home. His days as military commander were officially coming to an end.

Beside him Harper stood as loyal as ever and put a hand on his shoulder.

"Thank you," he said. Casper looked at him and smiled.

"For going home or for Isis?" he joked lightly. Harper smiled and shook his head, then he looked back at Casper and shrugged.

"A little bit of column A, a little bit column B," he replied. Casper shook his head.

"Come on, Romeo, let's go get some dinner."

"Right behind you," Harper said. Casper stopped and looked at him with all seriousness.

"I know," he said. And he did, he knew Harper was his backbone, his ally under any and all circumstances. His best friend for life, and the one man who'd truly been with him for everything. Together they would head home, riding into the proverbial sunset like so many heroes had done. But Casper knew the only real hero was the man beside him, overcoming so much adversity, Harper truly was a better man than he.

Their voyage had been going for several hours, and they were just a few more hours from the rip when suddenly the ship jarred to a halt. Casper had been in his quarters resting, but the second it happened he jumped up and dropped into a full-out sprint to the bridge. When he got there he was out of breath and couldn't say a word, he simply sat in the captain's chair, praying the halt hadn't meant what he thought.

"Freddy?" he managed.

"I can't explain it, sir, but...oh no..." Casper knew what the exclamation had meant and knew they were in trouble. He was trying to catch his breath while ordering the crew to raise shields, but he never got it out. Before he could say a word a sensation ran through his body and he knew he was being taken from his ship again.

When he was back in one piece he looked around the dark room and knew exactly where he was. This couldn't be happening again! Not now! Casper was infuriated!

"*You bastard*!" he screeched into the darkness. *"Show your hideous face, so I can kick it in!*!" The exertion was great and he sank to his knees suddenly overcome with helplessness. He'd never see his friends or family again thanks to this monster that held him.

Just then the door opened. Casper was ready for another onslaught of malicious beatings but instead, two guards came in, lifted him to his feet and moved him through the halls of the ship. This time Casper saw much more than he had originally, he saw many individuals in fundamentalist uniforms who watched him closely as he was marched past.

Casper, though tempted to try and run, was held too much in awe at the technology the ship possessed. It crushed him to think the fundamentalists had superior technology than the fleet. It was a kick in the behind, but Casper refused to show intrigue while others were watching.

Finally he was brought to a room where a man stood looking out a large window. That man was Atkinson. The guards shoved Casper to the floor then disappeared when the door closed.

"You animal..." Casper got up and was about to charge Bernard when suddenly the man spun around holding a small control panel. He pushed a button and pain shot through every inch of Casper's body. He stumbled, lost his footing, and crashed into a nearby table.

"Easy now, Prince, you didn't really believe I'd let you in here without a back up did you? My doctors gave you more than just a pathogen you know." Bernard smiled.

"What…?" Casper gasped, but he couldn't get the sentence out. He wanted to know what was causing the pain. Bernard smiled and got to Casper's side holding the button still.

"A nice little micro-organism that responds to a certain frequency, *this* frequency, nasty little thing isn't it? It's called a Falarkian Curse Worm, aptly named from his home origin and the effect it has on those blessed with its presence," Bernard explained. Then he stood up and released the button. The pain stopped and Casper was finally able to pull himself into a nearby chair. Bernard sat across from him and pushed a plate of fruit toward him. "Hungry?" he asked. "Or perhaps something to drink?" Casper sat perfectly still and silent for a moment taking deep breaths and eyeing the man.

"Why would you not just kill me?" Casper asked. Bernard smiled.

"Right to the point I see, but all in good time, my friend, you should eat, wouldn't want you to pass out before we arrive," he replied.

"Arrive where? And what did you do with my ship?" Casper hissed.

"Your ship is fine, on my honor you are the only one I have taken this time," Bernard replied.

"'Cause that means a lot," Casper snorted. He was going to say more, but then he realized how dangerously close Bernard's hand was getting to the control panel. Casper wouldn't be able to take another run with that thing so he quieted down. Bernard saw this and smiled even more, God how Casper wanted to knock that stupid smile of his face.

"You're learning quickly, this is good," Bernard said. Then the man leaned forward, closer to Casper. "Tell me, Prince, what did you think of our technology?" Casper kept his mouth shut, any answer would lead to that button being pushed. So instead he remained silent, unfortunately for him that silence didn't save him as he'd planned. Bernard pushed the button and held it for several seconds. Flashes of pain danced across his eyes as he curled into a tight ball. However, as soon as it had begun it was over. Bernard looked very pleased with himself. "Okay, Prince, maybe I should lay down some ground rules for this little conversation before you die faster than I had planned," he said.

"Yes, let's," Casper said through gritted teeth, "because clearly I don't know them." Bernard let out a low bellowing laugh and slapped the table startling Casper slightly.

"My apologies." Bernard laughed. "So here is how this is going to work. I'll ask you questions and you respond; otherwise, you get a jolt. You start getting too smart and you get shocked. You try and run, you get shocked possibly shot by the guards outside. You try and contact help, you get shocked until the situation is remedied. Say something I don't like, you get shocked. Something that isn't the truth, and you get shocked. I'll let you ask some questions *if* I think they are appropriate, otherwise…"

"I get shocked, I get it," Casper finished. "Basically you can find reason to use that button for everything I do." Bernard developed a wry smile and nodded.

"You *are* a quick learner. So as per my earlier question? What do you think of our technology?" Bernard asked.

"I think individuals like you shouldn't have that kind of…" A jolt, this time a powerful one right up and down his spine and temporarily blinding him in pain.

"Forgotten the rules already?" Bernard asked when it was over. Casper shook his head and wiped the drool that had dripped from his mouth when it was frozen open in pain.

"It's impressive," Casper whispered.

"I knew you'd like it!" Bernard slapped his hands together. "It's also what's going to finally destroy your horrible dictatorship over many of the planets letting my way of life free."

"To do what? Kill everyone who opposes you? And you call *me* the dictator?" Casper growled. He had barely closed his mouth when the Falarkian Curse Worm jumped into action again and Casper could barely move.

"What did I tell you, Prince?" Bernard asked. "Are you going to try and have a civilized conversation or must I return you to your cell and those brutes out there who get their jollies from hurting the weak such as yourself?"

"I'm sorry…" Casper pained.

"Pardon?"

"*I'm sorry*!" he yelled. The pain stopped and Casper opened his eyes. At some point, he had fallen onto the floor out of the chair. That's where he was now with Bernard looking down over him.

"Now where were we?" Bernard asked as Casper clawed his way back into the chair. He refused to show that Bernard was breaking him, he got into the chair and tried to sit tall and defiant.

"I believe we were talking politics," Casper replied as strongly as he could. Bernard smiled and shook a finger at Casper.

"You are right, Prince Hawk, thank you," he said. "What you will soon witness, is the death of your politics and the new way of life. I learned something when I worked with your brother on those diplomatic missions. I learned that politics is a very dirty business, you can never count on individuals to do what you want. Everything is so complicated, so you know what I did?" Casper hesitated to answer but when he saw Bernard moving his finger to the panel he jerked at the sheer thought of that pain.

"I don't know, what?" he quickly responded. He was relieved when Bernard's finger moved away from the button.

"I started a war," he said simply. Casper was confused, how would starting another war change the way of life they had been living for so many years. "Come let's look out the window, shall we?" Though it was extremely difficult Casper managed to get to his feet and lean on objects to get himself to the window. His blood ran cold at what he saw, a war had indeed unfolded between the fundamentalists and *Casper's own squadron!*

Casper could see the *Nautilus* weaving and dodging along with all the other ships, weapons' fire going every which way and that. After watching it unfold for a bit Casper turned to Bernard.

"What makes this battle so special?" he asked. Bernard smirked as he stared out hungrily toward the warring ships but didn't look at Casper.

"In ancient Greece of the old planet Earth, there was a story that lasted throughout the ages. Men fought for one purpose; all the armies of Greece and their kings set sail to fight one battle for one cause. Never before and never again did time know such brutal slaughters or rage-filled contests. Do you know what that story was?" Bernard asked. "Do you know why so many men lost their minds and saw no other remedy than to fight one of the greatest wars ever fought?" Casper didn't know, he had studied ancient Earth and the many cultures that came from it but the particular story Bernard was referring to he did not know.

"What?" he asked. Bernard then looked at him.

"It was the battle of Troy in the Trojan wars, they fought mercilessly for Helen of Troy, King Agamemnon's wife whom the young Paris stole from him…The greatest war was fought for one reason. love," Bernard explained. Casper was still confused, so he looked out over the warring ships again and tried to piece the information together. He looked down at his feet briefly and when he looked back up he was a bit startled to find Bernard staring at him so intensely. "You, Prince Hawk," Bernard said. He waved out over the ships and then pointed a single finger at Casper's chest. "They are all fighting for *you*," he said.

Casper's mouth dropped open. Suddenly he understood why this battle was different. Bernard knew as did Casper, that the royal family of Hearth Condes would never allow such a personal attack to go unpunished. They'd think and act simply on emotion. Their allied forces seeing such dismay at the main joining force between them all would undoubtedly join in and fight as well.

Bernard had probably destroyed any diplomatic solutions, as those who fought for love fought for their way or no way. In the end, only one side would prevail and with the technology Casper had seen on Bernard's cloaked ship, he wasn't so sure the fleet would come out on top.

"Oh god," Casper breathed. He slunk to the floor. The plan, if it wasn't so horribly evil, was absolutely flawlessly perfect. Bernard laughed and then sighed.

"Genius isn't it?" Bernard smiled. "And you won't find your god here. You know there's no way with what you've seen that this battle will go in your favor. Politics be damned, you want something, you fight for it and take it." Casper was too shocked to speak, a war, an all out war between humanity was being fought not for religion and power like always but rather for *him*.

This couldn't be happening—his friends, his colleagues, his allies, all for him. Casper could see all their faces, all the men, women, and children who had ever smiled at him and waved hello.

"So why not just kill me?" Casper finally asked in a small voice. Bernard reached down and pulled Casper back to his feet, facing him out the window, forcing him to look at the battle scene.

"Do you really think the Greeks would have gone after Troy if Paris had simply killed Helen? They would have found Paris and killed him, but the fact that the loved one was still alive brought them out to get her back," Bernard explained. Casper was overwhelmed with emotion at the moment and if it weren't for Bernard pressing him against the window he surely tumble over.

"That's why you infected me and let me return?" Casper whispered.

"Precisely, dear prince and now, I've taken you back because I didn't want you to miss this," Bernard said. "Years later when you and I are remembered, it will be because of this, the Greeks had Helen of Troy, I have Casper Marseille Hawk of Hearth Condes."

"No…" Casper said weakly. Finally Bernard released Casper and he slid to the floor again, this time no longer able to keep a stoic face, tears rolled down his cheeks.

"Oh don't be so dramatic," Bernard sighed. "After all you should be happy, it may last for a bit but once this war is over there shall be peace for thousands of years! Casper, think of the lives you are making better by being such an intricate part of this war." Casper snapped his bloodshot teary eyes up toward the man and narrowed them.

"All I can think about are the thousands maybe millions who will die in the name of *your* madness!" he hissed. Casper expected

Bernard to press the button and waited for the shot of pain to ride through him. Oddly enough it never came. Casper opened his eyes and saw Bernard holding out a hand to help him to his feet again. Casper refused the hand but got to his feet with the aid of a nearby table.

"I had a son once too, you know, he'd be a bit older than you now, but close," Bernard said. He motioned Casper back over toward the chairs they had been sitting at, but by now the war was still in full view from anywhere in the room.

"Where is he now?" Casper asked. He wondered if Bernard's son was as insane as his father.

"Sadly, he's dead." Bernard sighed. The smile had gone from the man's face and a genuine look of heartache showed. "I loved that boy with all my heart, then one day he got sick. The doctors tried but no one could do anything to save him. This was when I was back on Hearth. I prayed to god every day and every night, begging him to spare such an innocent boy. In the end, your god refused my prayers and my boy died a painful slow death. That's when I knew that the fleet's way of life was a dying one, humanity can't rely on god to protect them, they have to protect themselves."

"Why are you telling me this?" Casper asked. He had become slightly intrigued with the story but still confused as to its purpose.

"Because I want you to know that your god doesn't exist, and pray though you may, he will not save you from your fate. Yes, lives will be lost, but it's all for the greater good of peace," Bernard responded. Casper thought about it for a moment and then looked back over to Bernard.

"So your son's death was necessary? Is that what you're saying? My slow death is a must like his was? Or are you just taking an eye for an eye?" he asked. Bernard stood up and headed toward the door not really answering the questions.

"Believe what you want, Prince, but try not to think about it too much, none of that matters now..." Bernard replied. Just as the door slid open Bernard paused and looked over his shoulder. "His name was Thomas." Then Bernard was gone as the doors slid shut. Casper rushed toward them hoping to get out but knowing there was no chance.

He pounded at them for awhile and screamed obscenities, but he knew his cries fell on deaf ears. Finally, he made his way back over to the window to watch helplessly.

Some ships of both sides floated mercilessly adrift in space while others still zoomed around them as if they weren't even there. Though the squadron was putting up a good fight, she was slowly losing. Casper managed to spot the *Nautilus* again and watched her move; he could almost feel Danielle and Isis fighting hard to stay in the battle.

He could hear Danielle barking orders left right and center and Isis feeding more power into the engines to get the ship moving faster. He prayed, even though it seemed futile, that the *Nautilus* would carry his princess home safely, even if it meant he'd never get closer to her again like he was now.

Casper sunk to the floor and wept for the sake of humanity because that's what humanity was doing for him. So much so did he want his mother's soothing arms and pretty voice to hum him to sleep. His body wanted to let go but somehow his mind kept him attentive to the fight.

As he watched, he got angrier and angrier. He knew he couldn't give up so soon. Bernard had been right, politics be damned, you want something you had to take it. If Casper ever wanted to see his loved ones again and stop this madness, he'd have to stay alive long enough to do it. The only problem was, what could he possibly do in his condition?

Casper was trying to devise any sort of plan a couple hours later after witnessing one of his ships get badly damaged and spun off into space, when Bernard returned. The smile on his face was as annoying as ever.

"Have you seen the new arrivals?" he asked. Casper raised an eyebrow, then slowly he turned to the window and his heart sank. A new squadron was approaching the fight: *Centaury Alpha*, the

Marquise's ships. No doubt headed off by Captain Emile Lawrence, a friend and fellow soldier to Casper's father. Casper sighed, they had come so quickly. "So it begins," Bernard said proudly. He turned back to the door when Casper realized something—of the fifteen-ship squadron, five had peeled off and were heading directly for the ship Casper was on.

At first it didn't make sense, how could they have known he was there? But then it dawned on him, Danielle, she had remembered and told the Marquise, so she could make it look like they were losing the battle. She was brilliant! A mastermind! Now the Marquise would be catching the cloaked ship and any others completely off guard.

"Indeed it does, Atkinson," Casper said. For the first time in days he smiled a genuine smile probably just as annoying as Bernard's had been toward him.

Bernard turned and frowned when he saw the five ships open fire. Seconds later the ship violently rocked side to side throwing both men to the ground. Casper knew he might get killed, but that fate had been sealed a while ago. He didn't fear death anymore, now he was grateful to be able to have such a feeling of reckless abandon. As he was tossed to the floor, he laughed despite the pain.

"You really thought my soldiers were that stupid??" Casper howled. "This battle is nowhere near done!" Bernard was getting to his feet and seemed to be searching for something. It was then Casper realized he wasn't holding the panel anymore. Now was Casper's chance. Just as Bernard located the thing and reached for it Casper ran over and crushed it under his foot. That was one problem solved now for the next one.

Casper lifted Bernard and punched him square in the nose letting the man flail back into the wall.

"*Smile now bitch*!!!" Casper howled. It was almost like he had been taken over by a certain animalism. It would seem that death was not a factor to care about anymore so Casper had gone wild. He grabbed some shattered glass from one of the most recent attacks by the Marquise's ships and lunged at Bernard pinning him to the ground and held the glass to the man's throat.

"You'd like me to kill you, wouldn't you?" Casper laughed. "Make it so simple for you to get out of this mess you've created!"

"My salvation will come!" Bernard shot back.

"*From who*??" Casper howled, his eyes were wide like a rabid animal now. There seemed to be a surge of adrenaline in his veins. "You have no god you heathen!" he bellowed. "And I'm going to make sure you live to see my people triumph over yours!"

"You've lost your mind," Bernard snapped. Casper hauled him to his feet and shoved him toward the door.

"You'd like that, wouldn't you? Actually things have never been clearer!" Casper laughed. When the door opened the two guards were getting to their feet from yet another blast. When they saw Casper and Bernard they reached for their weapons but Casper stopped them. "Uh uh boys, drop your weapons or I kill your leader," he ordered. The two guards looked at each other and then to Bernard.

"Do as he says," Bernard said as Casper pressed the blade deeper into his neck drawing blood. The guards dropped their weapons and backed off. Casper managed to pick up one of the weapons and use it instead of the glass.

"Not so tough now are you?" Casper sneered. Bernard said nothing, so Casper jammed the gun into his back. "You know how this works, say anything and I shoot you. Where's the shuttle bay on this thing?"

"You really think I'm going to…" Bernard never finished. Casper shot in him the foot and then leveled the gun at his crotch.

"Next shot is going to sting a whole hell of a lot more if you don't start talking," he said.

"Oooooooooooooooooooooooo!" Bernard wailed in pain.

"*Where is it*!?!?!?" Casper screamed at him.

"Deck forty-two! F-section!" Bernard pained. Immediately Casper sprung into action. He used some nearby junk that had come loose in the last assault to tie Bernard's hands together and then made the man move toward the lift.

Due to the confusion and lack of a leader, the fundamentalists were running around like chickens with their heads cut off. Several explosions rocked the ship, and Casper could only guess one of them hit the engine relays. No one seemed to notice Casper as he strode past with their leader at his mercy.

"So much for loyalty," Casper joked as they moved.

"You can't ruin my plan! It's perfect!" Bernard wailed as they reached the shuttle bay.

"Already have, Atkinson besides you of all people should know the plan wasn't perfect! It was based on emotion! That is even worse than politics!" Casper snarled maniacally. He was almost to a point where every explosion that rocked the ship made him giddy. As they headed to one of the few shuttles left in the bay the computer's voice came over the com.

Evacuation recommended, ship's systems in total failure, destruction in fifteen seconds...fourteen, thirteen...

"Well, we better get a move on then!" Casper laughed.

"You're crazy, you've lost your mind!" Bernard said.

"That may be, or maybe your pathogen did something to my brain! Or maybe it was one too many Curse worm shocks! *Who cares! I feel like a new man!! come on, Bernard, let's go for a ride*!" Casper howled again. He practically threw Bernard in the back of the shuttle and secured him to one of the chairs. Then he jumped to the pilot's chair and flipped the shuttle on.

Seeing no other option Casper blasted the bay doors and swooped out of the bay moments before the huge explosion colored the sky.

"WHOOOOOOOOO HOOOOOOOO!" Casper exclaimed pumping his fists in the air.

Suddenly the fun of the moment was gone as a piece of debris smashed into the stern of the shuttle sending her tail spinning out of control. Casper tried to get hold of the controls and stop the violent spin but it was no use, they were headed directly for the thick of the battle. A collision was most likely going to occur, with whom was the only question.

In a last ditch effort to salvage the shuttle, Casper shut down all engines and gave a short burst with the port bow of the ship. The ship shuddered violently. Casper almost thought his move was going to rip the ship to pieces but was relieved to find it had worked.

Granted every system but life support had been pretty much fried, but it didn't matter, they had stopped.

"You really think anyone out here is going to pay attention to a tiny little shuttle with no power?" Bernard asked. Casper didn't respond, he simply leveled the weapon to Bernard's knee and fired. Bernard roared in pain and clutched his bloody knee.

"I am doing my best to not kill you right now, so you'd better just keep your damn mouth shut," Casper said. He went back to the controls in front of him and pushed the com key.

"This is Captain Hawk of the Centaury Zebra Squadron, I require assis..." Casper was mid-sentence when the shuttle lurched forward slightly. Looking out the main screen Casper saw a tow line had just attached itself to the hull. Watching further still Casper could only smile as the *Nautilus*, damaged as she was, was reeling the shuttle in.

When the shuttle was aboard the *Nautilus* Bernard was immediately taken into custody and Casper was loaded onto a stretcher. All the adrenaline he had coursing through him was suddenly gone and he felt as weak as a kitten. The moment he walked out of the shuttle he collapsed into a nearby soldier's arms and was quickly transported to the infirmary.

In the infirmary things only got worse as Casper could barely sit up under his own power. The doctors were rushing about to try and get fluids and nutrition into him and trying to transfuse blood to keep him conscious when Danielle came rushing into the room. She ran to his side and clutched his hand.

"You did it," she said. "The fundamentalists are in retreat now that their cloak is gone."

"How did you know I was out there?" Casper croaked.

"Harper sent a subspace message, he told me you had been taken again and then I remembered the cloaked ships you told me about. Moments before the Marquises got here I told them and the rest is history." Danielle smiled. Casper sighed and nodded his head tiredly.

"Good, it's over," he said.

"Yes, we're heading home!" Danielle exclaimed. "And that's not all—the doctors on Hearth say they have something that should reverse the pathogen. You just need to hold on." Casper smiled at the idea but then his smile faded, he didn't have the energy.

"I'm so tired," he whispered. Danielle clutched his hand even harder and closed the distance between them. Through his blurred vision he could see she had tears in her eyes.

"You promised me you'd hold on, you can't break that promise, Casper," she said. Casper felt awful, but there was nothing he could do.

"I know, I'm sorry, forgive me," he whispered.

"I won't! Damn it, I won't!" Danielle exclaimed. "You can't die because you aren't forgiven! Casper, I love you!" It was the last thing Casper heard before a rush of static hit his ears and things began to darken.

"I'm trying, forgive..." but he never finished, everything went dark.

He was eight years old as he stood on the deck of the largest fleet transport which was arranged to carry the funeral procession of Harper's mother. Casper saw Harper with his face buried in Patricia's arms. Next to them was Anthony and Harper's father Paul. Paul looked like he wanted to cry and couldn't be simply settled by the comforting hand Anthony rested on the man's shoulder.

Casper understood that Harper's mother was gone and wasn't coming back, but he didn't exactly understand why. As people paid their respects to Harper's mother Casper turned to Maverick who stood beside him. Maverick had to know the answer; he was, after all, eleven years old.

"Hey, Mav," Casper said quietly. Maverick turned to him and raised an eyebrow.

"Why did she die?"

"She was sick."

"I know that but...*why?*" Maverick shrugged.

"Sometimes God calls his people back to him before their time.

He wants them to come work for him because he has a special job for them." Maverick's answer made a little sense, but Casper was still slightly confused.

"Why couldn't we all go?"

"He didn't need all of us."

"What's the special job?"

"Guardian angel."

"Really??? Cool!"

"Not for Harper or his dad." Casper looked over at Harper still in Patricia's arms hiding his tears as his father stroked his son's back gently.

"But why would god take her now? Why wouldn't he let Harper and his dad say goodbye?" Maverick paused for a second and then shrugged again.

"Sometimes you don't get to say goodbye, it's sad but…that's what happens." Casper could see it really hurt Harper and his dad not to say goodbye and felt bad. Then he tugged on his brother's sleeve, again Maverick looked at him.

"What if we don't get to say goodbye?"

"What?" Maverick seemed off guard with the question.

"You, me, mom and dad? What if we don't get to say goodbye?" Maverick looked away from Casper and back to the procession.

"Then I would be sad too, just like Harper and his dad."

"Do you think we'll get to say goodbye?"

"Dunno."

"Mav, will you miss me?"

"Don't be stupid, of course, it's what families do when a member dies."

"I know but…will *you* miss *me*?" Maverick turned to Casper and this time faced him straight on.

"Yeah, Cass, I will. Even though you're a pain sometimes, I'd miss having you around to beat up." Casper sneered at his older brother who smiled and ruffled Casper's short hair.

"I have another question," Casper said.

"I'm not going anywhere," Maverick said.

"What does a guardian angel do?" Casper asked. Maverick looked around for a bit then raised his hands.

"I guess they protect people they love, kinda like a ship's force field, except a guardian angel uses himself to protect you. They have super powers too. They can be anywhere and everywhere they want to be just so they can be with you. Not only that, but they have the power to speak to you." Casper's eyes bugged out of his head with wonder.

"How???" he asked incredulously. Maverick poked Casper in the chest right where his heart is. "Whoa," Casper said, looking where Maverick had just poked him.

"Yep, pretty neat huh?" Maverick asked.

"I'll say, so...Harper's mom is still kinda with him isn't she?" Maverick paused again and then smiled.

"Exactly," he said. Casper was so happy with his new revelation and knew he had to share it with Harper and his dad. Casper started to move away from his brother and walked over to Harper and the others. He didn't know if he was supposed to talk to them at that moment, but he knew Harper would like what he had to say. Gently Casper tugged on Harper's pant leg and his mother's. Patricia put Harper down subsequently drawing all the adults' attention to Casper.

"Guess what Mav just told me? You're goina like it," Casper said. Harper wiped his eyes on his sleeve and then looked at Casper.

"What?" he asked.

"Your mom is still with you, but she's a guardian angel now with super powers and whenever you wanna talk to her you can! Just make sure you imagine her close to your heart," Casper said.

"Really?" Harper asked. His friend looked slightly intrigued by this new information.

"It's true! Mav told me and he's eleven!" Casper replied. Harper walked over to his dad with a smile on his face.

"Did you hear that, Dad? She's still with us!" he said. Paul looked down at his son and then to Casper, tears were glistening in his eyes. At first Casper thought he had done something wrong, but then Paul smiled and got to his knees between the two boys looking at Casper.

"You're a smart little boy, Prince Casper," he said barely above a whisper. "Thank you." Casper didn't see that he had done anything amazing, he simply told the truth.

"You're welcome." He smiled. Paul pulled his son into a hug and Casper turned to look up at his parents. Anthony picked Casper up so he was at eye level with the two of them. "Did I do something good?" he asked, not totally sure what was going on. Both his parents smiled at their boy and hugged him.

"Yes, Casper, you did something very good," Patricia replied. Casper didn't know what but he was getting praise nonetheless. He looked over his dad's shoulder to Maverick who gave him the thumbs up. Casper smiled, he didn't like it when people were sad and glad he could help if only a little bit.

Drip, drip, drip, drip, drip. Water? Did something spill? Where was he? What was going on? Wasn't he supposed to be dead? No, death wasn't this...this...alive. So where was he? *Open your eyes stupid and find out.* Casper obeyed, he opened his eyes and at first was assaulted by a bright light. He snapped his eyes shut again not wanting to experience that again. *Don't be such a baby, it wasn't that bad, you still want to know where you are don't you?* Casper obeyed again, this time it wasn't so bright.

Casper looked around him, he recognized this room, it was *his* room! He was back on Hearth Condes in his own bedroom. *Now to find the source of that damn drip, so I can get back to sleep.* Casper looked around and then found the drip noise, it came from the IV in his arm. *How did that get there?* Casper was slightly dazed, still he decided to get up and find out what was going on.

Fortunately the IV pole provided for a good crutch as he moved over to the balcony window. *Drip drip, drip, drip. More drips!* It was raining outside and it made everything look dismal. Casper planned an about face and a retreat back to his bed. He had made it half way there when his door opened. A woman, probably a nurse, judging by her clothing came in carrying a tray of medical supplies.

However, when the woman saw Casper, her eyes bugged out of her head, she dropped the tray and ran from the room. The clattering sound drove spikes of pain into Casper's head. *Was that really necessary?* He climbed back into his bed and noticed someone had left fruit on his bedside table. *Don't mind if I do! Man, I'm starving!*

Casper was contentedly munching away on some grapes when Maverick and his parents appeared in his doorway. Instantly Casper knew something wasn't right, they were the same people, but they looked…different. Patricia had a hand over her mouth as if she was looking at a ghost. Anthony was just as stunned. Maverick in a uniform above the status Casper had last seen him in and with longer hair stared at him in utter disbelief.

Casper slowly put down the grape in his hand so as not to scare them away and finished eating the one in his mouth. When the grape was down he cleared his throat and smiled nervously.

"Kay, you're freaking me out," he said. His voice didn't sound his own, it sounded weak and scratchy as if he hadn't spoken for a long time. Patricia was the first one to move; she came up beside Casper and pulled him into a hug and wept into his shoulder. Casper was startled by this but hugged her back nonetheless. "Hey it's okay, Mom, I'm alright, don't cry," he soothed. Then he looked up at his dad and Maverick. "What's going on?" he asked. Finally Maverick managed to clear his throat and speak while pulling up a chair for Anthony.

"Cass…there's no easy way to say this…you've been in a coma for almost eight months now," he said quietly. Casper was shocked silent. He looked off into the distance and then down to his mother's sob-wracked body.

"Eight months?" he breathed. Maverick nodded. His father who was sitting took Casper's hand, but his father was still speechless.

"Yeah, the doctors on the *Nautilus* managed to keep you alive until you got back to Hearth, then the doctors here gave you the antidote, but you had already slipped into a coma," Maverick explained. "Man, Cass…it's good to hear your voice." Casper smiled weakly.

"It's good to be awake," he said.

"You don't know how much we love you, son," Anthony said, the older man had finally found his voice. Casper smiled and squeezed his father's hand while still hugging his mother. His mother brought her face away from Casper's shoulder and looked him in the eye. Her face, flushed with tears, still managed to let a smile beam through.

"My beautiful, beautiful boy," she said. "I'm so happy you're alright! I love you so much." Casper smiled back warmly and kissed his mother on the forehead.

"I love you too, Mom," Casper said. Then he looked to the rest of his family. "I love you guys as well." Maverick put an arm on his father's shoulder. It was truly a bonding moment, all those years of feeling distant gone in this one moment. Here they were together as a family.

"It's true!" Casper looked up from his family to the doorway where Harper stood with a huge smile on his face. He came in the room to Casper's side and put a hand on his shoulder. "You gave me gray hairs, I counted, three, THREE," Harper joked. "It's good to see you smile man, you have no idea." Casper let out a short laugh but then he realized something.

"Where's Danielle...and Isis?" an overwhelming fear came over him, the last he saw of them it was in the middle of a space battle.

"Don't worry, they're coming...slowly," Harper smirked. Casper was confused,

"Slowly? Why what's wrong with them? Why do they need to move..." When Danielle and Isis appeared in the doorway, Casper's mouth nearly hit the floor and his eyes bugged out of his head. "Holy Moses," he gasped.

Danielle who was being helped along by Isis was quite, *quite* pregnant. Casper was stunned to no end as Anthony gave up his seat for the woman. Casper was still dumfounded and positive he looked like an idiot with his mouth hanging open.

"Dani..." he said. "You...you're *huge*! I mean...you're *gigantic!*" Everyone in the room laughed lightly even Danielle who looked exhausted.

"Not the best thing to say to a pregnant lady, Cass," Maverick snorted. Casper was still too shocked to speak as Danielle took his hand and placed it on her stomach. Casper felt something move and retracted his hand in shock.

"You woke up just in time…after all I wasn't about to raise our daughter by myself," Danielle said. Just when he thought it wasn't possible, Casper's eyes grew slightly larger. He pointed at her stomach, then to Harper for confirmation after pointing to himself. Harper nodded with a laugh.

"It's all you, man," he said. Suddenly it clicked. He was alive, and better still, he was going to be a father.

"ALRIGHT!!" he exclaimed. The room again burst into laughter mixed with tears of joy.

EPILOGUE

Days later Casper sat at his usual place at the banquet table, the smile hadn't disappeared from his face. Every day since he had awoken had seemed better than the last. As things were explained to Casper he was told that Bernard had been tried and put in prison for the rest of his life on a prison planet for the fleet. More still the fundamentalists had scattered throughout the universe because of the lack of a leader and the fact that the fleet tracked down and destroyed all cloaked ships ridding them of the upper hand advantage.

As it turned out the Marquise people had shown up in the nick of time because Maverick had asked them to follow the fleet a day after Centaury Zebra had taken off. Freddy and Linda had been ecstatic when Casper and Danielle had shown up on the launch pad a day or two ago and brought everyone's attention to them. As an added surprise in a joint effort with Captain Lexis and Isis, the squadron had brought back and fixed the *Spartan*. A gift that which nearly brought Danielle to tears in happiness.

Since he had been in a coma his mother had stepped down from sovereign ruler officially giving the title to Maverick, so she could devote her attention to sitting at Casper's bed side. It was a simple gesture but to know his mother was with him the whole time humming her sweet tune, let Casper believe it was her support that pulled him through.

Upon news of his good health the wheels were set in motion for a banquet in his honor, *his* honor. The banquet was supposed to happen five days ago save on little issue, Danielle gave birth to a beautiful baby girl. Their beautiful daughter, named appropriately after someone who meant a lot to the two of them, was blessed with a rare genetic sight anomaly: one blue eye and one brown. The doctors say it was because of the residual effects of the pathogen but nothing to be concerned about.

Now five days later mother and daughter sat right at Casper's side, as the small child was peacefully sleeping. Casper couldn't have been prouder as he looked at them and winked. Danielle blew Casper a kiss and turned her attention back to the sleeping bundle.

"Ladies and gentlemen of the court…" It was weird to see and hear Maverick get up to address the court and all its patrons but Casper had to remind himself that a lot could happen in eight almost nine months. "It is my pleasure to welcome you all here on such a wonderful, happy occasion. Not only is Prince Casper awake and healthy, but so is his newborn baby girl. I'd like to introduce you all to the newest member of the Hawk family: Isis Elizabeth Hawk." Applause rose up from the hall and then quieted down.

"So in honor of this wonderful occasion, tonight's ceremonies will be opened up to the public court yard for all the city to take part in." Again a cheer rose up from everyone in the room.

Later that night Casper and Maverick stood outside sipping some champagne together when Isis and Harper came up to them with Danielle.

"Should you be drinking that?" Harper asked.

"Hey, I'm a father and I'm alive, someone once told me to live in the moment," Casper smiled. The group laughed and the baby started to cry.

"Uh oh, someone's ready for a little food." Danielle smiled. "I'll see you all inside." Casper gave her a heartfelt kiss before she brushed her hand against his cheek and left the group. As he watched her go he caught something out of the corner of his eye, Harper and Isis's hands were tightly intertwined.

"I see I'm not the only one who's happy," he said. Isis looked away sheepishly and Harper smiled nervously.

"We weren't sure what you'd say," Harper said.

"I couldn't be more delighted." Casper smiled. "Congrats."

"I take it that means you'll be my best man?" Harper asked. Casper laughed and nodded.

"I meant to thank you and Danielle, Casper, it's an honor you named your girl after me." Isis smiled. Casper took her hand and then hugged her.

"None of this would be possible without you, I'm just glad you've found happiness again," he said.

"Did the doctors say if baby Isis was one hundred percent healthy or not?" Harper asked. Casper sighed, it had been the only unresolved issue of the miraculous recovery.

"They say she's healthy now, but it's too soon to tell if there are any lasting genetic effects," Casper replied.

"I'm sure it will all turn out for the best." Isis smiled. Casper nodded, hoping and praying she would be right. Then Isis and Harper said goodnight and took leave, hand in hand, and yet again Casper and Maverick were alone.

Casper looked up to the star-filled night sky and took a deep breath of the crisp clean air.

"I'm glad we didn't have to say goodbye," Maverick said. Casper looked at him, he too was looking up at the stars but how could he possibly have known what Casper had dreamed about in his coma.

"Pardon?" Casper asked. Maverick looked at him.

"Harper's mom's funeral, I never forgot that conversation. Something I should have added. It's nice to be able to say goodbye, but I'd rather *not* say goodbye at all," he replied. Casper though about it and then smiled.

"Amen to that," he replied. Maverick pulled Casper into a headlock hug and ruffled his hair then pulled him into a normal hug.

"I'm glad you're okay, Casper."

“Call me, Cass, Casper sounds so…*old*.” Maverick and Casper laughed with each other and then continued to watch the universe unfold above them. It was a beautiful night and turning out to be a beautiful life.

The End

Printed in the United States
31464LVS00001B/493-510